THE HUNTER'S POTION

THE PARANORMAL COUNCIL #8

LAURA GREENWOOD

Visit Laura Greenwood's website at:

www.authorlauragreenwood.co.uk

www.facebook.com/authorlauragreenwood/

The Hunter's Potion is a work of fiction. Names, characters, places, and incidents are the products of the author's imagination or are used fictitiously. Any resemblance to actual persons, living or dead, businesses, companies, events, or locales is entirely coincidental.

The Hunter's Potion was previously titled *Witch's Potion*

What if you used a love potion, then met the love of your life?

Mia has been lusting after her next door neighbour, Skyler, for months, and has finally decided to do something about it. But when Felix, the best man at her sister's wedding, shows up, she realises it might not be Skyler she wants after all. With a love potion in the mix, and her sister's insistence on marrying the wrong man, doesn't Mia have enough to worry about?

-

The Hunter's Potion is part of the Paranormal Council series and is Mia & Felix's complete romance.

1

THE INVITATION STARED at Amelia from where it was pinned to the fridge with a novelty magnet. She hated it already, and it'd only arrived a few weeks ago. A bit late for a wedding invite, but then that was just what her older sister, Rebecca, was like. She was getting married and Mia's gut was telling her it was a bad idea. It wasn't even that Mia thought Robert was a bad person, though he had his moments, it was more that she didn't think he was right for Bex.

But that wasn't even the worst bit. The worst bit was that she didn't have a date. And the wedding was tomorrow. She'd have to endure the entire thing while being asked when it was going to be her turn, and being told that she'd have to find a man of her own. And *that* didn't sound fun. So she'd come up with a solution. Not a very good one necessarily, but a solution all the same.

Pulling her Grandma's old potion book from the shelf, she flicked to the page she'd earmarked years ago, but promised herself she'd never use. There, in her Grandma's elegant script, were the instructions for making a love potion. One so strong, that a single drop would have the other person head over heels in an instant. She'd had all of the ingredients ready for weeks, ever since she'd first considered using it. She even had an item that the man in question loved. Well, kind of. She had petals from one of his flowers, and as a proud gardener, her neighbour Skyler definitely loved his plants. Or at least she hoped so.

Mia chewed on her lower lip, unsure about whether or not to go ahead with her plan, but the moment an errant thought about how her cousins would react when she turned up alone again, she made up her mind. They wouldn't be purposefully cruel, but with Luke recently mating with a tiger shifter, there was next to no chance that she'd get away unscathed.

With a glance at her cauldron, she scooped up the book and the ingredients that she needed, before making her way over to the low table she kept next to her open fireplace. Maybe it was stereotypical for her to have a cauldron in her kitchen, but she wasn't all that good at actual magic. Potions were definitely her specialty, and for that reason, she'd required her house had an open fireplace. It wasn't just potions she was good at either, it was anything that involved mixing things up. She worked at a chemist, making medicines from plants. She wasn't the only paranormal to work there either, though she hadn't let on that she knew one of the other scientists was more than just a human, it wasn't her place to.

She concentrated on her hands, picturing the flames in the grate. She may not be good at magic, but she could at least do the basics like this. They sprung to life, licking the bottom of her cauldron as they heated the water that she'd left in it overnight. She turned her attention away, reading through the instructions again to make sure she knew what she was actually doing, and then picked up the first ingredient. She worked through the instructions one by one, double checking to make sure she was doing it right. She probably didn't need to do that, she was a natural after all, but it reassured her knowing that she was following her Grandma's instructions to the letter. This wasn't something she wanted to get wrong, not when she was going to give it to someone she was pretty sure was human. There was a chance of it going really badly, Faye had once managed to turn her best friend into a toad when they were younger. Luckily Reese was a shifter, so knew about them anyway, and he'd understood in the end, but it still didn't go down all that well.

After completing the final step, and scattering the flower petals into the potion, it turned a light glittering blue, which presented a problem that Mia hadn't really considered, how on earth was she going to get Skyler to drink it when it didn't look at all drinkable. Sighing, she waved her hand in the direction of her kettle, hoping that her magic would behave and just turn it on. The tell tale sound of boiling water relaxed her slightly, and she went back to her plan.

It was quarter to seven and Skyler would be out in his garden for the next half an hour or so, and with the air rapidly cooling, despite it being summer, it would be the perfect time to offer him a coffee. All she needed was a drop of the potion anyway, and it was supposed to be sweet, so slipping it in would just replace the sugar he normally had. Mia smiled to herself. The plan was foolproof, and something even she could be proud of.

She poured the water into two mugs, adding

coffee to his and tea to hers, before leaving them to brew. Now all she had to do was work out how to get the potion into the coffee without creating too much of a mess. Inspiration struck, and she pulled a shot glass out of her cupboard, almost skipping over to the cauldron in her excitement. She dipped the glass into the blue liquid, filling it to the top, and carefully walked back over the the drinks. With as steady a hand as she could manage, she tipped a few drops into the coffee, and watched as it swirled through as it mixed in.

Trying not to burn herself, she picked it up and pushed through the door that led outside, and to the fence between her and Skyler's properties.

"Hi Mia," he said as he spotted her. He stood up straight and wiped the sweat from his brow, making Mia salivate, he looked particularly yummy like this.

"Hi, I was making a brew, and thought you might like one. Dark and sweet, just how you like it." Just like she was. She didn't add that, even though she wanted to.

"Thank you," he said. Their fingers brushed as he took the mug from her, and she made sparks ignite on her fingertips. She'd heard that that was what happened when witches met their one true love. Or mate, or whatever the hell it was called for them. For some odd reason no one ever seemed to actually know what it was called. But she wanted it to happen, and maybe if she sparked it off, then something would take. Unfortunately, all she got from Skyler was a bland smile...though that would all change once he'd drunk his coffee.

2

Felix woke early, as he should on the day of his best friend's wedding. It wasn't every day that the notorious player he'd gone to school with got married. Truth be told, he felt kind of sorry for Robert's fiancée. Rebecca seemed like a genuinely good person, and she was shackling herself to someone with questionable morals. Felix didn't even know why the two of them were still friends really, except that he wanted to at least try and keep Robert on the straight and narrow, even if it was a lost cause.

A knock sounded on the door of Robert's flat, where he and the other groomsmen had stayed the night before. As was customary, Rebecca, or Bex as she'd insisted he called her, had stayed at a hotel so that the two wouldn't see each other today. Felix actually kind of hoped that she'd get cold feet and not go through with the whole thing. He felt oddly protective of the woman, almost to the extent that he felt protective over his younger sister, Autumn, who he'd always kept far far away from his friends. He didn't trust them around her.

He moved over to his overnight bag and withdrew a bracelet made of willow bark, slipping it around his wrist. He was already risking it by spending almost two days away from his tether, he didn't want to take the risk of not having anything of it on him. Though he realised that it could draw some interesting questions later on.

The knocking intensified, the person on the other side clearly impatient to get in. "Alright, I'm coming," he said, just loud enough that he knew the other person could hear him. The incessant knocking stopped, and he made his way over to the door before it could start again. Robert and the other groomsmen had gotten drunk the night before, and the last thing he wanted to deal with was their grumpiness if they woke up to pounding headaches.

Oblivious to the fact he was only wearing pajama bottoms, he swung the front door open to be taken off guard by the most beautiful woman he'd ever seen. She was only wearing a pair of leggings and a baggy pale yellow jumper with her dark hair tied back in a ponytail, but there was something about her that just called to him. Her dark brown eyes met his, and they held each other's gazes as something passed between them. Neither of them spoke a word, and they didn't need to.

"Hi," the woman said softly ,as if not wanting to disturb the peace that had extended between them. "I'm Amelia, Mia I mean. Bex's sister." Her rambling was adorable. Yet another thing that took him off guard about this woman. She was nothing like the type he normally went for. Maybe he'd have to change that.

"Erm, hi, I'm Felix, Robert's best man," he introduced himself, pushing his hand around the nape of his neck in a fit of nervous tension. He really needed to pull it together, if a pretty woman was all it took to get him tongue tied, then he was really going to have problems at the wedding later. According to Robert, most of Bex's friends were 'bangable'. Though with Robert, it was sometimes hard to tell what his standards were.

"Can I come in? I need to grab some stuff for Bex," the woman, Amelia, no Mia, asked.

"Sure." He stepped away from the door and Mia's eyes roved down his bare chest, taking in every inch of the muscle he'd worked hard for.

"Stop it, Mia. Remember Skyler," she muttered under her breath, tearing her eyes away from Felix's chest. He smiled to himself. He didn't think that he was meant to have heard that. But who was Skyler? He didn't like the sound of the other man already and he hadn't even met him yet. After thinking on it, he decided he didn't like the idea of any man near the pretty brunette. He cleared his throat, trying to use the action to clear his thoughts.

"What do you need?"

"Oh just some personal items she forgot." Mia waved a dismissive hand which he took to mean that Bex needed underwear, or some other kind of feminine grooming product. He wouldn't pretend to know much about it. She made her way to the door to Robert and Bex's room, and it wasn't until her hand was on the door that Felix realised that she couldn't go in there.

"No," he almost shouted. She turned back to him, a frown marring her face.

"What?"

"You can't go in there, I don't know what state Robert's in." He hoped that was enough to put her off going in. Truthfully, he wasn't sure if Robert was even alone in there. He probably was, but it wouldn't be the first time he'd been with a woman that wasn't his fiancée. Robert really was an idiot. Felix had no idea how he could sleep around on someone like Bex. She was beautiful, talented and successful, all the things a man could want in his life. It was all he really wanted. Well, right now all he really wanted was the woman in front of him, but normally it was.

Her mouth made a perfect little 'o' as she realised what he was saying, and her hand dropped away from the door handle.

"Would you like me to get it for you?" She nodded.

"Pink and blue bag, should be by the side of the dresser, but she's not sure. She wanted to come herself, but..."

"It's bad luck. And you don't want to push it."

"Especially when she's a..." He looked at her curiously, but all she did was shake her head, which just made him wonder what she'd been going to say even more. He looked her up and down again, partly to take her in again, and partly to try and ascertain if she was something more than human. He came up blank. Though he wasn't sure how he'd be able to tell unless she had some obvious characteristic. He'd heard that some of the fae had odd tattoos, but he couldn't see anything on her pale unblemished skin. What he wouldn't give to trail his hands over it...he shook his head, trying to rid himself of the inappropriate thoughts.

"Are you going in?" Mia asked, and it was only then that he noticed she'd stepped away from the door completely, leaving the way open for him. He sighed, and closed the gap, brushing past her as he did. The air almost felt like it was heating around him, and he frowned. Maybe she was some kind of elemental? He'd thought they were solely a legend that humans had made up to explain away weird things witches had done, but maybe not.

Slowly, he opened the door, not quite knowing what he was going to find on the other side. Luckily, Robert was alone. Though he was sprawled out naked on the bed, which wasn't a pretty sight. Something inside him felt extremely satisfied that he hadn't let Mia come in. She shouldn't have to see that. He looked around, and quickly located the bag that she'd mentioned. He grabbed it, not wanting to stay in the room with a naked Robert any longer. It wasn't anything that he hadn't seen before, but that wasn't the point. Some things shouldn't be shared.

He exited the room to find Mia pacing back and

forth, and blatantly ignoring the other passed out groomsmen that littered the room. They all looked extremely worse for wear, and he was relieved he wasn't in the same state himself. It wasn't a good look for someone's wedding day. Not in the slightest. And not when there were going to be pretty bridesmaids in attendance. Maybe he'd even get to walk down the aisle with Mia. Now there was a weird thought. And it wasn't just of how she'd look in a bridesmaid dress either. Instead, it was how she'd look wearing a white dress and veil of her own. He was suddenly very glad that no paranormal he knew of could read minds. He still didn't know if she even was one, but it didn't hurt to be safe.

"Here," he said, passing her the bag. Their fingers brushed and he could have sworn that he saw a few errant sparks where their skin touched. He shook his head. No way was that possible. He was a dryad, that just wasn't how their kind worked. Unless...he pushed the thought away.

3

MIA LOOKED at herself in the full length mirror in her sister's bridal suite, and had to admit that she looked good. Gone were the leggings and oversized jumper she'd been wearing earlier, replaced with a gorgeous jewelled gown that fell to the floor in a waterfall of glittering fabric. At first, she'd been hesitant to wear it, but after the insistence of her sisters, she felt better about it. That wasn't to say that she didn't feel a little over exposed still, she did, the mostly see-through fabric couldn't hide enough skin for her, but she knew it was what Bex wanted. Faye looked equally as stunning in her own version of the dress, her blonde hair such a contrast to her elder two sisters.

"Mia, do you have it?" Bex asked from where she

was having her makeup done. It was the kind of thing that they could have done themselves with minimum effort, especially as Faye had long ago perfected the art of applying make-up with magic, but they'd decided against it. Bex had wanted the entire wedding experience, and that meant no magic today at all. Well, other than the love potion that Mia had already slipped Skyler. There was no way she was risking it wearing off in the middle of the wedding. That would just cause a scene.

"Yes." She opened her bag and pulled out the worn velvet jewellery box she'd put there earlier. She opened it, taking in the long gold chain with a crystal pendant swinging from it. It'd been their grandmother's, as had the other two that matched it, and would stay in their boxes until the day that Mia and Faye met their other halves. Mia had almost been tempted to forget the trinket, and use that as a sign that Bex shouldn't be marrying Robert, but the thought of how upset her sister would then be stopped her. And the last thing she wanted to do was upset her on her wedding day. Mia snapped the box shut before handing it to Bex. She was supposed to open it herself, as was tradition according to their Grandma. Bex pressed the latch on the box, and nothing happened. The box didn't open for her at all, which was odd. Mia hadn't had any problems with it.

"Why isn't it opening?" she asked, tearing up ever so slightly as she tried to open the box again.

"I don't know."

"You opened it." She looked up at Mia with unshed tears shining in her eyes.

"Leave us please," Mia said to the hair and makeup artists that were in the room. They hastily dropped what they were doing, leaving the three sisters alone in the cluttered room. It was unfortunate, but they couldn't really discuss magic while there were normal humans about.

"What was it that Grandma used to say?" Faye said softly from her seat by the window. Mia glanced over, and was unsurprised to see that her sister had her eyes closed as she soaked up the afternoon sunshine through the glass.

"That they were for us, the blue box was for the first, the green for the second and the red for the third," Mia cited off. She'd been the closest to their Grandma, and she'd heard the instructions at least a dozen times a week growing up.

"What if it doesn't mean our birth order?" Faye opened her eyes and looked sympathetically at Bex.

"What else could it mean?" Bex asked.

"Maybe it's the order we meet our soulmates in," Faye suggested. She added a shrug as the others looked at her.

"But I met Robert years ago." Mia said nothing. Neither did Faye, and the silence stretched on until it gained an uncomfortable edge. "Great, so the two of you think that Robert isn't the one for me?"

"It might not even be that, maybe I just met my soulmate sooner and didn't realise?" Mia suggested, trying to keep her voice soft and placating. She might not like Robert, but she wanted her sister to be happy. "Maybe it's just a case of getting the other boxes and trying those?"

"That's not a bad idea," Faye said. "Did you bring them?" she asked her. Mia shook her head.

"I didn't think we'd need them." Faye grabbed Mia's arm in a surprisingly firm grip and dragged her away from Bex, who seemed lost in thought.

"We need to get those boxes, she's not going to accept anything until we do. Where are they?"

"At home."

"Is there anyone who can go get them?" Mia started to shake her head, before changing her mind.

"Felix," she said, before she'd even realised whose name she was saying Really, her choice should have been Skyler. He was the man she'd come here with after all. But instead her mind was filled with thoughts of the tall dark and handsome, not to mention shirtless, man from earlier in the day.

"Who the hell is Felix?" Faye demanded.

"The best man."

"And you know him how?"

"I don't really," Mia said, shrugging.

"Hmm." Faye looked lost in thought. "Fine, go send him then." It took a moment for the words to register in Mia's head, but once they did, she began questioning what the hell she'd let herself in for. She had all of ten minutes experience with the man, trusting him in her house wasn't something she'd imagined possible.

4

THE LAST THING Felix expected was to open *another* knocking door to find the bride's sister standing on the other side of it. She was a lot more put together than last time, with her dress glittering in the light and her hair nearly pinned. Weirdly, he couldn't decide which look he actually liked more. They both suited her.

"I think it's bad luck for you to be here," he said, leaning against the door frame and giving himself another moment to take her in. She really was beautiful. Not merely sexy or pretty like he normally thought about women either, but drop dead, out of this world gorgeous. He wanted to take her as his own at the same time as hiding her away from the world so no one else could look at her. Which wasn't normal for a dryad, he'd never heard of any of his kind becoming possessive before.

"No, it would be bad luck if my sister were here and if Robert saw her. I'm just a bridesmaid."

"One dangerously near the best man," he muttered and she cocked her head almost as if she'd overheard. But that couldn't be right. Only a paranormal would be able to hear the volume he'd spoken in, and even then not all of them would.

"Look, I need a favour. It's for the bride."

"And I'm just supposed to say yes?" he rose an eyebrow to accompany his question, and she scowled at him, which didn't take anything away from how she glowed in his eyes.

"Please Felix," she said, a vulnerability entering her voice that surprised him. He didn't take her for the kind of woman who just let that kind of emotion show.

"Fine, if it's for the bride."

"I need you to go to my house and get the two jewellery boxes that are on the dresser in my bedroom."

"You want me to go to your house? Into your bedroom? As in, where you sleep?" Even as he asked, his mind went to what other activities she'd get up to in her room. And what they could do there together. Maybe after the wedding he'd see if he could convince her, though he had the feeling that once the two of them started, there would be no end. It wouldn't be the worst thing really.

"Yes, look I wouldn't ask if it wasn't important. But we were given these necklaces by my Grandma and I brought the wrong one because we thought that Bex would be the first..." she trailed off, looking horrified and he had to wonder why.

"The first what?"

"Nothing," she shot back instantly, convincing him that there was definitely something going on here that wasn't quite normal.

"Fine. What do they look like?"

"This," she said. She held out a worn oblong box. "Just please don't try to open one." He frowned, that was odd to say the least.

"Why?"

She glanced away, refusing to meet his eyes. "Just, it's special that Bex is the one that opens it is all." She finally met his gaze again, and her eyes bore into him. Damn, he was a goner. He'd do anything for this woman and she didn't even know it.

"Okay, have you got your keys?" She handed them over, along with a slip of paper with her address on.

She'd come prepared then, as if she knew he'd cave.The moment that their fingers touched, he felt tingles spread through him, but ignored them. It was just his overactive imagination making her into something that she wasn't. "I'll bring them by the Bridal suite when I get back."

"Thank you." The words were quiet, but he could tell she genuinely meant them. With a nod, he strode off down the corridor and towards where his car was parked. There were still a couple of hours before the ceremony, but it was probably better that he got a move on and back with the necklaces, they seemed to mean something important to Mia, and he didn't want to let her down.

The drive didn't take very long, and he pulled up in front of a tidy house with a white picket fence. Somehow he wasn't surprised. The house was dark, and it was clear that the owner wasn't in, and, interestingly enough, the house next door looked the same, except that there was still a truck parked in the driveway making it seem as if there should be. Felix got out of the car, slamming the door shut and fingering the keys that Mia had handed to him. He didn't know what it was about the situation, but something about it seemed right. He should probably just go with it, sometimes that was the best way when it came to paranormals. He knew that.

He turned the key in the lock and opened the door, taking his first step into the home of the woman who was fast becoming his new obsession. The house was surprisingly tidy, and he found himself wandering through the downstairs rooms until he came to the kitchen. It was large, with an open fire place and cauldron as the central focus, completely at odds with the modern appliances that lined the kitchen sides. Actually, it was completely at odds with just about everything he'd guessed about Mia. Curious, he moved towards the fireplace, noticing that there was open book perched on a table next to. It was clearly old, the hand written looped handwriting only adding to that impression. He read the open page, his eyebrows raising as he did. If he wasn't mistaken it was a recipe for a love potion, but that would mean…

A wide smile passed over Felix's face. That meant that Mia was likely to be a witch, which could completely explain the way he was feeling about her. Maybe he'd finally found his one. Or maybe she'd used the love potion on him. His eyes widened and his heart rate quickened as he realised what that could mean, or at least they did until he realised he hadn't eaten or drunk anything in Mia's presence. So if not him, then who had she used the love potion on, and why was he feeling this way? So many questions, and he was looking forward to uncovering the answers.

5

MIA BIT HER LIP. She hated to admit it, but she was worried about whether or not Felix would manage to bring them the necklaces in time, and even more worried about whether either of the other two boxes would open for Bex. She hoped so, she didn't want her sister to be disappointed. Which made her wonder. The first box had opened for her, which was weird. She'd have thought that it would open for Faye if it was about who met their mate first. Everyone knew that her and Reese were meant to be together, even if they barely touched in public. She'd have to remember to ask her little sister about that later on. Or maybe she could share the love potion trick with Faye to speed things along a bit. So if the first wasn't Bex or Faye, that meant that it was her that had met her mate already. Her thoughts strayed to Skyler, with his tanned arms and dark blonde hair. Maybe she'd been too hasty with the love potion, maybe he was already hers anyway. At least that was what the necklace said. Carefully, she withdrew the box from her clutch, not wanting Bex to see and wonder what she was up to. She pressed the catch and was almost surprised to find the box opened for her again. Part of her hadn't expected it to. The same long gold chain and crystal lay against the worn velvet. It was pretty, there was no doubt about that, but she wasn't convinced it was anything to be upset about. She didn't even have the urge to put it on.

A knock sounded on the door, startling Mia out of the slight trance the necklace seemed to have had her in. That was just odd, why was it affecting her like that? There was nothing magical about the necklace itself after all, just the box that it came in. Her Grandma had always been a little eccentric like that.

"Will you get that?" Bex asked, sounding a little nervous to Mia's ears, but that was to be expected on her wedding day. Or apparently so. Mia didn't think Bex should be nervous. She was a witch for Christ's sake, she should know that she was marrying her one, not just guessing like she was with Robert.

"Yes," she said, rising to her feet and making her way steadily to the door of the Bridal suite. Hopefully it would be Felix and he'd be delivering the other two boxes, putting her sister's worries at ease. She swung the door open and her heart sank as she took in the tall blonde frame of Skyler standing on the other side. She tried to convince herself that she was happy to see him, but for some reason that just wasn't happening and disappointment was the predominant emotion going through her.

"You look beautiful Mia," he said in his low voice, and Mia caught an intrigued look from Faye who was sat across the room. She shook her head slightly, hoping that her sister would realise that meant it wasn't Felix and that they didn't have the necklaces yet, but the confused look said Faye didn't quite get it.

"Thanks," she muttered, still trying to muster up some excitement over the man she'd been lusting over for months. She caught herself. Since when had she thought about it as lusting after and not loving from afar? "What are you doing here?" she asked.

"I came to see if you need anything." Mia glanced

at her older sister who was almost shaking and made a split second decision.

"Vodka."

"Sorry?"

"Can you get us some vodka please?" she asked, receiving only a perplexed nod in return. That wasn't right. Felix would have made some wisecrack about how they shouldn't be drinking before a formal event. Wait, no, that wasn't right. How would she know what Felix would or wouldn't do? She barely knew the man. Why was he even part of her thoughts anyway?

"Yes," he said, giving Mia an awkward half wave as he walked away from the suite and down the corridor. Hopefully he'd be back soon, but if not, at least he was busy and not completely abandoned.

A firm grip closed around Mia's wrist and she felt herself being dragged to the side of the room, finding a very confused looking Faye squaring off with her.

"Who was that Mia?"

"My date."

"Felix?"

"No, Felix isn't my date. That's Skyler," Mia answered quickly, but even so she found herself enjoying the way Felix's name felt on her tongue.

Like it fit there. Like he fit there. She shook her head to rid herself of thoughts like that, knowing they wouldn't get her anywhere.

"You've never mentioned him before," Faye prompted, putting a hand on her hip and giving Mia a spill-it-now look, just like the one their Mum used to give when she was angry with them.

"He's my neighbour." Mia shrugged. There wasn't really anything else to say. It wasn't like she could admit to Faye that she'd used a love potion on the man, her sister would never understand. She had no real reason to considering that she already knew who her mate was.

"And you brought him because..."

"I thought there was something there."

"Did the necklace box open for you before today?" Faye asked, a thoughtful look on her face. Mia stared at her, shocked at the seemingly sudden change in direction.

"I don't know, I never tried it."

"Have you ever wanted to open if before today?"

Mia thought back, humouring her sister ever so slightly, but not knowing what the hell she was getting at. "No."

"But you met Skyler before today?"

"Yes, we've lived next door to one another since I moved in."

"Hmmm."

"Whatever you're thinking, you're wrong," Mia said defensively.

"You don't even know what I'm thinking."

"That the necklace means something. It probably doesn't, Grandma probably just put a spell on it so that it would open on a certain date just to confuse us all. Maybe if we asked Grandad nicely, he'll tell us when the other two open." Mia took a breath, surprised at herself for saying what she had. She'd never thought things like that about her Grandma before. Then again, she'd never had a reason to. .

"If you believe that then I'm a tree climbing goat."

"Like that's a thing." Mia snorted.

"It is, they live in Morocco and eat nuts out of trees, but that's not the point. You don't believe that about Grandma, I know you don't, so just stop pretending already." Faye gave her a stern look, and Mia kind of had to admit defeat. Her little sister could be terrifying at times.

"The alternative is accepting that Bex hasn't met her mate yet," Mia whispered hastily, hoping their older sister wasn't paying any attention. "And that you and Reese aren't meant for each other. Or that I met my other half at four," she added. An odd look crossed Faye's face as she considered.

"Me and Reese are complicated," she said in a small voice that made Mia wonder if there was something more to her concern. She placed a consoling hand on top of Faye's, hoping that it would convey what words couldn't. "It's fine we're dealing with it."

"If you want to talk-"

"I said it's fine," Faye snapped, before sighing. "I'm sorry, it's just difficult at the moment. I know he's it for me, but every time we get close to touching, even if it's just holding hands, it feels so wrong we have to stop."

"And he's definitely it?"

Faye nodded instantly. "He's it. It's just weird. And I'm getting a bit tired of it all. I mean I'd quite like a first kiss at some point." She looked so sad that Mia longed to give her a hug, but she couldn't without raising Bex's suspicion. She had enough to worry about today.

"I'm sorry Faye, if there's anything I can do-"

"There isn't. But thank you. Is that how you feel about your Skyler? Is he definitely it for you?" Mia took a mental step back. She hadn't thought about it like that at all. She liked Skyler she supposed, but as the morning passed she'd realised she wasn't thinking about much at all. Unlike a certain tall dark haired man. Nope, now was not the time to think about Felix. Not at all.

"I don't know," she admitted eventually.

"Then maybe he's not it. Who have you met recently that could have changed how the box reacted?" Faye asked, flipping from the emotional woman of moments ago to the logical thinker that she was. Mia's immediate response was to say Felix, but she wasn't ready to admit that aloud. She'd deal with him when she had to.

"No one." Faye raised a questioning eyebrow, clearly not buying it in the slightest.

"Hmmm."

"No one, Faye."

"We'll see." There was a twinkle in her eye as she said it, a clear sign that she thought Mia was deluding herself. And maybe she was, but it was Bex's wedding day, now wasn't the time to sort out her love life. Which was ironic given that just yesterday she'd planned for it to be just that.

6

FELIX HALF-RACED THROUGH THE HOTEL. He was already picturing the smile on Mia's face when he presented her with the jewellery boxes. They'd been exactly where she'd said they were, and after discovering she was more than just a human, he hadn't felt the need to snoop around her house as much. There was no need when he was safe in the knowledge he'd be spending a lot more time there soon. In Felix's mind, there was very little doubt about what she was to him. The only problem was that she obviously hadn't come to the same conclusion, especially if she was using a love potion on someone. Why would she even do that? She was gorgeous, no way did she need to trap a man to her side, they were probably falling at her feet as it was. And *that* thought wasn't a pleasant one. Definitely not.

A soft thump left him reeling, and he almost fell to the floor, just catching himself with a steadying hand on the wall. He looked down to find the dark haired object of his most recent thoughts looking up at him with a wide-eyed innocent stare. He could get used to that. Though he would bet almost anything that she wasn't as innocent as she first appeared. That seemed impossible.

Her hand was pressed against his chest, the heat of it almost searing his skin through his shirt and he had to resist the urge to take it in his own. That would be too much for her. He was going to have to win her round slowly, though all he really wanted to do was back her against the wall and have done with it.

"You're back," she said, her voice soft and breathy. If she kept this up then she was going to be the death of him.

"I said I would be," he replied, equally as soft, giving off the impression that they were actually having a lovers' moment and not their third conversation to date.

"I know, just -"

"And we're on a deadline right?" A small crease

formed on her forehead, and an adorable expression crossed her face. "Your sister's wedding," he prompted. Her mouth opened, making a perfect 'o' shape.

"Sorry, I-" She frowned and cocked her head to the side. "I don't know how I forgot that." She shook her head as if trying to chase something away.

"I get it." And he did. There was definitely something happening between them, and it was all he could do to remember his own name, never mind the fact he was at a friend's wedding. He stopped cold as realisation hit. No wonder Bex and Robert didn't seem right for one another. Robert was as human as they came, and if Mia was a witch then that meant that Bex was too. She wasn't meant to be with Robert because Robert wasn't her mate. This wedding could go horribly horribly wrong if that was the case, and he didn't want it to. The last thing he wanted was for Mia to be upset because Bex hadn't had the day of her dreams.

Neither of them moved, and Mia's hand still pressed against his chest, leaving them connected in a way that he'd never felt before. There was definitely something about her that he just couldn't get past, and if he was honest, he didn't really want to.

"Would you like them?"

"Huh?" she asked, her eyes flicking to his lips, making him long to close the distance between them and kiss her like he wanted to. It'd be the most intense kiss of his life he was sure.

"The necklaces. Would you like them?"

"Oh. Yes, please."

He handed her the two boxes and she took them, her hand leaving his chest and leaving him feeling a little bereft at the loss of contact. She studied the top one for a moment before pressing the catch and frowning as nothing happened.

"Was it supposed to open?"

"I guess not," she responded, a confused look on her face. "What made you ask that?"

"It didn't?"

"No, I mean why aren't you questioning why it didn't open?"

"Oh, well you're a witch right?" She looked at him, shocked, then nodded once.

"How-"

"You left you spell book out by the fireplace."

"And you looked?" It sounded like she was supposed to be sounding shocked, but failed miserably. Instead she sounded a little bit in awe.

"You could hardly expect me not to, Mia." He liked the way her name sounded, the feel of it on his lips almost as delectable as kissing her would be. Maybe it was what he should settle for for now. He'd have to do the kissing part later. Maybe after she got a few drinks in her and forgot whatever man she'd used the love potion on.

"So why aren't you freaked out?" She looked adorable. Confused but intrigued. He liked it. Though that was hardly surprising, he seemed to like everything about her.

"Did it cross your mind I might not be just human too?" He said it slowly, not sure how she was going to react, but when she didn't say a word, he pushed his sleeve back, revealing the bark bracelet he'd put on today. If anything would convince her then this would.

"You're a dryad?"

"Yes, how did you know?" he asked, surprised that she'd caught on so quickly. His kind tended towards secretive.

"I've heard stories about how dryads take part of their tethers with them when they're away from it." She reached out and touched the bark gently, sending shivers through Felix. He hadn't realised how good that would feel. He wasn't even sure that she realised what she was doing at all. There was something magical about her touch, especially when light blue sparks began to dance over her fingers and the bark.

"Yes, I'm a dryad."

"What tree is it?" she asked, looking up at him again with her wide eyes.

"A willow tree."

"Where is it?"

"Back at my flat, in the kitchen." She laughed, a musical sound that lit up his heart.

"Does it have a swing too?"

He frowned. "No, why would it?"

"Well if I had a tree in my kitchen then I'd make sure that it had a swing on it, just for fun you know."

"Maybe I'll put one there for when you visit," he murmured the words, not realising just how close the two of them had actually gotten as they'd been talking.

"And you're assuming I will?"

"I'd never assume, it makes an ass out of you and me." She laughed again, and leaned that little bit closer. She was so close he could almost taste the sweetness of her lips. It wouldn't take much to kiss her now, and he was arguing inwardly about whether or not to actually go ahead and do it.

"But you want me to?"

"I've seen yours, you should see mine," he responded.

"That seems only fair."

"It does doesn't it?"

"But has anyone ever told you that you're incredibly cheesy?" she asked.

"No, they haven't." Despite himself, he lifted a hand and almost tucked a strand of hair behind her ear, but stopped himself just in time. He didn't want to freak her out too much. He did however, lean inwards, coming close to touching his lips against hers.

Which was when she freaked out, almost vanishing into thin air, which wasn't a normal witch power. He stood there, frowning in the direction that she must have gone, disappointed that things hadn't gone better.

7

No way had she come that close to kissing Felix. She was on a date with Skyler, the man she couldn't seem to forget up until today. And yet there she was constantly doing so.

She looked into the bathroom mirror, pinching her cheeks to try and make herself focus. Not that it helped, her traitorous mind kept going back to thoughts of Felix's lips close to hers in the moments before she'd pulled away. She wished she could splash cold water on her face, but ruining the meticulously done make-up wasn't an option, especially when she didn't have Faye's skills to magically reapply it. Instead, she locked the bathroom door and hoped that it would be enough to entice Squeak into an appearance. She guessed correctly., and the tell tale soft blue glow of her mouse familiar filled the bathroom. She held out her hand and Squeak ran up to it, nestling in her palm. It sounded ridiculous to anyone that wasn't a witch, but there was something about the appearance of her magical familiar that made her feel less alone. Probably because no one else would ever actually see Squeak, though her cousin Luke swore that he'd seen his best friend's familiar once. Mia wasn't sure whether to believe him or not, but she wouldn't be voicing that opinion today. It was best not to upset the wedding photographer, especially when he was bringing his new tiger shifter mate with him.

"Okay Mia, you can do this. No way is the dryad going to beat you." A dryad. Felix was a dryad. That opened up a whole number of possibilities that she hadn't even considered before. Maybe she was being as naive as Bex was with Robert. After all wasn't she the same in tricking a human into loving her? Did that make her a bad person? And why the hell hadn't she had these thoughts before. It would have been good to have considered these things before drugging Skyler. "Am I really a bad person Squeak?" she asked her familiar, only getting a faint noise in response. Well of course he wasn't going to answer, he was made of sparks.

Knocking pounded on the bathroom door. Damn she was fed up of knocking today, it seemed to be all that she was doing and receiving.

"Coming," she called out. She unlocked the door, a pang of regret going through her as she watched Squeak disappear. Not her mate on the other side then. He'd be the only other person to ever see her familiar. She opened the door to find Skyler standing in front of it, and dread replaced the regret. Well at least that one solved that question. But, just to be sure, she threw herself into his arms and kissed him. He kissed her back, and there was clearly passion in it, which meant that there was likely at least a little attraction on his side under the love potion, but that was all. She didn't feel the tingles that she'd felt when Felix had nearly kissed her earlier. Which could only really mean one thing.

She broke the kiss, giving him a weak smile that he returned with a lovestruck grin. At least her potion skills weren't under question she supposed.

"Your sister sent me," he said without adding anything else.

"Which one?" Not that it mattered, she just needed something to say.

"The blonde one."

"Faye," she supplied, already feeling annoyed that

he couldn't remember her name. It wasn't like she hadn't talked about her sisters before, and she'd given him the rundown on the way to the hotel earlier too.

"Yes, Faye."

"Did she say anything else?" she asked. Impatience now adding to the annoyance.

"Just that it was about time to start and that you needed to take your place at the end of the aisle." He shrugged.

"What about you?"

"I have a seat on the bride's side apparently." He didn't seemed bothered in the slightest, which was odd. Surely he should do considering she'd just kissed him, and he'd effectively being invited into such an important day for her family.

"Fine, let's go." They walked off, leaving the bathroom, and the kiss, far behind. It was all very odd. This wasn't how she expected a love potion to work. He should be doting on her surely? Instead he just seemed indifferent. Unless...maybe something about a mating bond superseded the love potion's magic. That seemed like the kind of thing that would happen. Except that it couldn't. If she accepted that that was a thing, then she had to accept that Felix was her mate, and she wasn't sure she was ready for that. Even if there had been sparks when she'd touched his bracelet earlier. She'd never sparked accidentally before. No. She had to stop thinking about this, otherwise it was going to take over her mind and completely ruin the date she was trying to have with Skyler.

8

FELIX WATCHED Mia from across the top table. It was nearly time for his speech and he was anxious to know how she'd respond. He'd had to keep it generic anyway, there was no way that he couldn't without revealing anything terrible about Robert. Or that he didn't think Robert and Bex were well suited to one another. He was even more sure of that now, which made him unreasonably glad that there was nothing personal in the speech itself. He didn't want to mislead the woman he was meant to be with into believing Robert was a good choice for anyone.

He tapped his spoon on his champagne flute, calling the room to silence and rose to his feet. At other weddings he'd been to, the groom was actually the one to kick off the speeches, but that didn't seem to be happening here. And Robert had said that Bex's Dad had refused to give a speech at all. Maybe he wasn't the only one to think this marriage was a bad idea after all.

"Hi everyone, thank you for coming to this special day of Bex and Robert's," he started, clearing his throat nervously. "It's really something to meet the one person that's meant to be yours forever, and it's something that should be treasured beyond everything. I remember the day that Robert told me he was going to propose. I was surprised, I think, but then I met Bex and it all made sense. She's a talented, beautiful and kind woman, who-" he stopped speaking. He didn't want to say that she deserved the happiness she was getting today. Partly because he didn't believe that Robert could provide it, but also because the bride in question didn't look particularly happy in the slightest. In fact, she looked as if she was about to cry. He glanced over at Mia who was watching her sister with concern and exchanging glances with the younger one, Faye he thought she was called.

"Sorry about that, something caught in my throat - emotion probably," he caught himself and the audience laughed. Pandering most likely, it hadn't been that funny. "Anyway, I was saying how wonderful Bex was and how she deserves as much happiness as could possibly come her way. Which I'm sure everyone that's ever met her can agree with. Robert's been my friend for a long time, and I can safely say that he is one of the luckiest men alive to have this woman as his own today. So, to the bride and groom!" He raised his champagne flute in a toast, and it took everyone a couple of moments to catch on that he was done. He supposed that was to be expected considering that his speech had been on the short side.

"The bride and groom," the room chorused. He glanced back across the table and his eyes met Mia's, something like understanding passing between them. She'd heard between the lines of what he was saying, he was sure of it.

The blonde man to her left whispered something in her ear and she almost batted him away, but didn't break eye contact with Felix. Interesting. From their body language he seemed a lot more into her than she was to him. Maybe this was the guy that she'd used the love potion on. But if that was the case, then why wasn't she more into him too? Unless it was something to do with the odd bond that seemed to be forming between the two of them. Felix almost grinned to himself, pleased that he seemed to be having an effect on the pretty dark haired woman.

9

MIA WAITED at the side of the dance floor having narrowly avoiding dancing with Skyler. Her interest in him was waning by the second and she needed to find a way to ditch him for good. Maybe then she'd stop throwing gooey eyes at the best man.

Felix was standing across the room and clearly trying not to look at her almost as much as she was trying not to look at him. Something was connecting the two of them and it was getting more and more difficult to ignore. If she wasn't careful then she was going to end up doing something stupid. Though on second thoughts, that sounded kind of fun.

Mia glanced around the room, making sure that she couldn't see Skyler. While he was still under the love potion she didn't actually want to hurt his feelings. Not seeing him anywhere, she weaved through the dancing couples, briefly noting how stiff and formal Reese and Faye seemed as they danced. She made a note to herself to see if there was anything she could do to help her sister and the shifter. They clearly wanted one another, so there must be some kind of block on them stopping them acting on it. But right now, she had something far more important to deal with.

She reached the other side of the dance floor and glanced up to see that Felix had given up trying to not watch her. Instead, his eyes followed her like a hawk as she approached. She thought about just jerking her head as a signal to follow her, but decided against it. She didn't want there to be any chance that he'd misunderstand her. Instead she reached him and grabbed hold of his wrist, dragging him towards the double doors next to the DJ booth. Felix didn't resist at all, and she quickened her pace. Now that she'd decided she was going to do this, excitement was building and she was desperate to get started.

They exited through the doors without anyone really noticing, and she turned left, down the corridor that contained a cupboard she'd spotted earlier. She could have taken him back to her hotel room, but then where was the fun in that?

Yanking the handle, she opened the door and pushed him inside, already reaching behind her to undo the back of her dress. Catching on to what she was trying to do, Felix's hands flew to the zipper at the back of her dress and slowly pulled it down-wards, his hand caressing her skin as he did.

"Aren't you worried someone will walk in?" he whispered. She shook her head.

"Are you?"

"Little bit," he said, chuckling. Mia smiled to herself before lifting her hand and letting her magic dance across her fingertips. Sending it out towards the door, she instructed it to lock, hoping that her weak magic would hold long enough to stop anyone actually opening. She had her doubts, but Felix didn't need to actually know that.

"Better?"

"Undoubtedly." He proved his word by pushing her dress off her shoulders and watching as it pooled into a heap on the floor. She shivered as the cold air touched her skin, anticipation building as she thought about what was to come.

She spun around to face him, finding that he was already shrugging out of his shirt and tie, letting them drop to the floor next to her dress. Their clothes would probably end up covered in dust, and showing the evidence of what they were about to do, but it felt too right for Mia to be able to ignore it. Fire burned in his eyes, and she couldn't resist a moment longer. Pressing her body against his, she kissed him for the first time. Yet it didn't feel like a first kiss. It felt like it was coming home and an explosion at the same time. Words couldn't describe how right it was. Felix slipped an arm around her waist, pulling her closer to him.

Her hands roamed over his chest, enjoying the feel of firm muscles beneath her fingertips. Trailing them further down, she unclasped his belt buckle and slipped it through the loops. She let it fall to the floor, anxious to return to her explorations, but Felix had other ideas. With two strong hands at her hips, he lifted her so that she was perched on the table of cleaning supplies that seemed to be sharing the cupboard with them, and stepped between her legs. He trailed kisses down her neck and she rolled her head back allowing him better access, ever so briefly regretting that he wasn't a shifter and wouldn't be biting her. As if he'd heard her thoughts, which was surely impossible, Felix grazed his teeth across her skin and she groaned loudly. If he carried on like this then she was going to find it impossible to hold back.

Felix slipped his hand between them, and moved it between her legs. She bucked against him, desperate for him to touch her. He chuckled, the sound vibrating along the length of her neck and she whimpered, it was all too much. She was sure she'd never survive more. Which was the moment that he pushed her underwear to the side and pushed a firm finger inside her. All of the doubts she'd had about him since meeting melted away. There was no way that he was anything but the one for her. The thoughts fled from her mind as he moved his fingers faster and as much as she was enjoying it, she needed more, and if the sparks that were dancing behind her eyes were any indication, her magic wanted more too.

Trying everything she could to focus past the sensation, Mia opened her eyes to find Felix looking at her with an intense look in his eyes, one that said much more than words ever could. She smiled lazily at him, before maneuvering her hands so that she could unzip his fly and remove the rest of his clothing. Then the fun could really start.

"Ah," Felix said, pulling his hand away from

between her legs as he flinched in shock. Panic flared behind her eyes.

"Are you okay?" Her voice came out huskier than she expected and she was rewarded with a heavily lidded look from Felix. He placed a reassuring hand on her thigh, and she was relieved that nothing serious seemed to be amiss.

"You seem to be sparking." He nodded downwards and she followed his gaze to where her hands were resting against his taut stomach.

"Oh." She pulled her hands away, trying to reign in the pale blue sparks that were dancing over them. But her luck had clearly run out, and nothing she was doing seemed able to stop them. To her surprise, Felix took them in his and pressed the back to the bare skin of his stomach.

"It's okay, it doesn't hurt. Just took me by surprise."

"You're sure?" She bit her lip as she looked up at him and he licked his own. He definitely seemed okay with that then.

"Yes," he whispered and she replied with a wicked smile. If he was sure, then she was going to have some fun.

Letting the rest of his clothes fall to the floor, she palmed him in her hand, letting the sparks continue to dance over them. Felix groaned, his head tipping back. She stroked him for a few moments more, but she was starting to get impatient, especially as there was no reason to wait any longer. With her free hand, she tugged on his arm to bring him as close as possible, feeling the heat of his body close to hers. Excitement was already building and he hadn't even entered her yet. That was about to change though, especially if she had her way.

She guided him closer still, until Felix took over, and pushed inside her, a sense of rightness filling her along with him. She soon lost herself in the rhythm and sensations, no longer paying any attention to the sparks that had spread along the rest of her body and were starting to cover Felix too. Nor was she paying any attention to the sweet smell of falling leaves as it filled the room. None of that mattered. Instead, she focused on the building pressure inside her and the warm hard man in front of her. All of a sudden, everything exploded, and a bright blue light felt like it filled the room as her skin tingled and Felix thrust one last time before groaning loudly. The two of them collapsed into a heap and she could safely say that she'd never been left so satisfied in her life. Especially not while in a cleaning cupboard.

10

FELIX TRIED NOT to look in Mia's direction again, and failed miserably. He'd been failing even before she'd dragged him off to a cupboard, so now he stood no chance. Not while he had the image of her with her head thrown back and sparks dancing over her pale skin branded on his mind. And oh, the sparks. They'd been like nothing he'd ever experienced before and he wondered why no one ever talked about being with a witch, especially if it was always like that. Though maybe it was only a one time thing, as disappointing as that would be. He'd have to ask Mia. She looked his way and their eyes locked across the now crowded dance floor. He was doing a truly terrible job at not looking at her then. Though the smile she threw him made it all worth it.

"Beautiful, isn't she?" A male voice broke through Felix's thoughts and he turned to find the blond man who'd been next to Mia at dinner stood to his side. Something told him that he needed to be careful here.

"Yes."

"I'm Skyler," the man introduced himself, though Felix noticed that he didn't offer his hand or any other form of formal greeting. Granted, they were at a wedding, so maybe a handshake would have been a tad formal, but he still expected there to be something.

"Felix."

"I know, you're the best man." He let the statement hang there, making Felix feel more and more uncomfortable by the second. He felt very uneasy about Skyler ever having been around Mia on his own.

"Yes."

"Have you noticed anything odd about her?"

"Mia?" he asked, taken aback. There was nothing odd about Mia. Unless he counted the sparks, which he didn't. He was pretty sure that with him, they were meant to happen. And was even more convinced by the promise of later she'd given him when they'd parted ways.

"You know her?"

"She's the bride's sister," he said, measuring his words as carefully as possible. Really, he could list the things that he knew about Mia on one hand. But considering one of those things was that she was his mate, he didn't feel bad about that. There'd be plenty of time to get to know her after all.

"Anything else?"

"No, sorry, I haven't noticed anything," Felix said, trying to clear his mind of any thoughts of magic.

"Let me know if you do." The man's voice was almost flat, and Felix began to worry about what was motivating him. If Mia had used a love potion on this man, then it had clearly backfired, and he didn't know whether that was something to do with her magic, or the man himself. He hoped the former, it'd be easier to deal with.

"Why?" he asked despite himself.

"I'm interested is all." Felix didn't find that ominous in the slightest. He had to warn Mia. Without tipping Skyler off that there *was* something different about her. Which could prove difficult. He wished he'd asked for her number, but being that they were at the same wedding for the next twelve hours, at a minimum, it hadn't seemed necessary. But how on earth was he going to get her attention without making it obvious. At the moment she was talking to an older dark haired woman who he guessed was her Mum, but he didn't know whether she was ready to tell her family about the two of them and it wasn't something he wanted to rush her into.

He tracked Skyler as he stalked around the room, seemingly watching Mia's sisters with the same intensity that he'd been watching Mia just moments before. Something wasn't right about the way he was being, and Felix knew that he needed to do something about it. Even if that something was just to warn Mia. He also needed to figure out if it was him that she'd used the love potion on, and why it wasn't working.

When he was sure that Skyler wasn't paying any attention, he made his way over to the bar and picked up two flutes of champagne, figuring that he'd get Mia's attention by handing her a drink. Hopefully the other one would go someway towards making him look good in her Mum's eyes too.

He weaved between the people, noticing Mia's blonde sister making eyes at a tall dark man who he'd seen her around for most of the day, but never actually seen touch for longer than a second. That was odd. They were acting like he wanted to around

Mia, and yet neither of them seemed to be doing anything about it.

When he reached Mia and her Mum, he took Mia's empty glass and placed it on the tray of a passing waiter, replacing it with one of the full glasses. He then handed the other to the older woman with a smile.

"Hi, I'm-"

"Felix. Yes, it's hard to forget the best man." She chuckled and he looked away slightly embarrassed. What was the point in being the best man if he wasn't able to stop her other daughter fro making one of the biggest mistakes of her life.

"Mum, Felix is-"

"Yes. I can tell." Mia turned bright red, though it could have been due to the alcohol rather than the embarrassment of what her Mum had insinuated. Felix slipped an arm around her back and placed a reassuring palm against her lower back. To his surprise, Mia leaned back into him and he only just managed to hold back the self-satisfied smile that was threatening to break out over his face. This woman did funny things to him, and he loved it.

"I'm a lucky man to have met Mia."

"Yes, you are." Her Mum chuckled again, looking pleased. "She's been alone for too long." He didn't know how to reply to that, but Mia tucked her head into the crook of his shoulder and he pulled her closer, offering her silent comfort.

"Mum!" she protested.

"Please, Mia. We all know you've been pottering around in that house for too long. Have you tried Grandma's necklace yet?" she asked. Felix felt Mia nod her head against his shoulder and wondered what that was all about, until he remembered the boxes he'd gone to get for her the other day. "Good, now I need to go see if my husband has managed to stay away from the cake." She tutted, but turned to leave, off in search of the slightly portly man he'd seen her with earlier.

"Are you okay?" he asked softly, almost completely forgetting about his concerns regarding Skyler. He was now a secondary problem, there were other issues that needed dealing with first.

"Shit," she muttered.

"Mia?"

"The necklaces. I didn't give the other boxes to Bex."

"Is that a bad thing?" She looked up at him, biting her lower lip in what looked like nervousness.

"No, I don't think so. The boxes won't open for her."

"Because they open when you've met your mate?" he asked, testing out a theory that had just sprung to mind.

"Yes. But how did you know?"

"A guess more than anything." He shrugged, trying to convey just how recent the revelation was.

"So you don't think they should be together either?" She glanced towards the top table where Bex was sat alone, slumped over her plate and pushing something around with her spoon, but not actually eating anything.

"No. I tried to talk Robert out of it-"

"But he wouldn't listen?" He shook his head. "Bex didn't either." She shook her own head, as if in disbelief that people could be so obtuse. They were so unsuited to each other that it was unreal, and yet neither of them actually saw it that way.

"I'm sorry," he said lamely.

"It's not your fault. Sometimes telling someone not to do something is the fastest way to make them do it."

"Like telling you not to kiss me right now?" She laughed, her face lighting up along with his heart. He loved that sound already.

"Do you need to tell me no for that to happen?" she asked, raising up on her toes and pressing her lips to his. He intended to only let it be a short kiss, but he soon forgot, and was kissing her almost as deeply as when they were in the cleaning cupboard. He'd need to stop soon or people would likely get a shock when the two of them carried on. Hell, they were like to get a shock when literal sparks began to fly. He pulled away suddenly, glancing down at a disappointed looking Mia, but thankfully not seeing any of the pale blue sparks that had been visible earlier. he was kind of disappointed.

"There's no sparks."

"I don't think they happen every time," she said softly, disappointing him all the more. She touched a hand to his lips and smiled slightly. "You know I can make them happen right?"

"You can?"

"I'd hope so. There's very little point being a witch if I can't do magic."

"So you're powerful?" She pulled a face and he wondered if it was a sore spot he'd hit upon.

"Not particularly. My skills lie in other arts." He waited for her to carry on, thinking he knew what she was going to say next. "Potions," she added after a moment.

"Love potions?" he asked, raising an eyebrow as he teased her. She whacked him on the arm softly.

"You looked!"

"I told you I did," he said, smiling down at her and enjoying the intensity of the moment. Something was playing at the edge of his mind, but he couldn't quite put his finger on what it was. Something linked to potions.

"Oh no." Her smile fell and her eyes widened.

"What?" he murmured, worried and already plotting a way to make the smile reappear on her face.

"I used a love potion on someone and I'm ignoring them." She looked well and truly horrified and he stroked a thumb over her lower back, hoping that it soothed her a little bit.

"Who did you use it on?" he asked, as the thing at the edge of his mind returned and he remembered what he'd come over to talk to her about. The longer she stayed silent, the more worried he got. As well as more certain that she was going to say the one name he hoped she wasn't.

"My neighbour."

"What's his name?"

"Skyler." The world at Felix's feet felt like it dropped away, that was the last name he wanted to hear.

11

MIA WATCHED as Felix's face fell. And she didn't think that it was because she'd said another man's name. No, there was definitely more to it than that, there was too much concern in his eyes for that.

"What is it?" she asked. Felix glanced around, worrying her even more. He grasped her arm and pulled her over to the side of the room, away from the eyes that might be watching. Hell, the eyes that were probably watching after that kiss. She wondered if the heat between the two of them would ever die. She hoped not, but she'd never actually considered that she might find the one person that awakened those feelings in her.

Felix pulled her into a shaded alcove, and she was kind of disappointed that he wasn't doing it for a more fun reason. Maybe later. Damn, she was becoming insatiable and she couldn't even help it.

"What is it?" she repeated, not at all reassured by the fevered look on his face.

"What do you know about Skyler?" he asked, his question taking her slightly off guard. That wasn't what she'd been expecting.

"He's my neighbour, moved in about the same time I did, he likes to tend to his garden." She shrugged, realising how little she actually knew about the man that she thought was it for her. That was weird, and not like her at all.

"And you used a love potion on him?" He looked down at her, his eyes filled with worry.

"Yes."

"Why?"

"I-I don't know. I thought he was wonderful and that it would get him to notice me, but now I don't know why I thought that was a good idea in the first place." Actually it kind of concerned her. She was normally completely aware of what was going on in her head. She was logical and methodical, hence the talent of potions. But none of this was any of that.

"Mia, I need you to think really carefully. Has he ever cast a spell on you or anything like that?"

"I don't know. I just know that I really liked him, and he didn't seem to like me. And then I gave him the potion and he agreed to come to the wedding with me and I was over the moon about it. But now-"

"Now it all seems a bit fishy," he finished for her and she nodded.

"Why are you asking?" She frowned up at him and he lifted a hand to her cheek, smoothing his thumb over her skin. She leaned into his touch, enjoying the warmth that had nothing to do with body heat.

"He was asking about you. Well, he was asking me if I'd noticed anything odd about you. Almost as if he expected you to have something different about you. I mean, beyond being drop dead gorgeous that is." She rewarded his cheesiness with a brief smile, and he returned it, seemingly relieved that she was still able to smile.

"But what does any of that actually mean?" she asked him. She was feeling more confused than ever, and not just because the way she'd felt about Skyler seemed to have completely changed over the course of the day. There was definitely something more going on, and it had her worried.

"Have you considered the option that he's after

you for something?" She laughed. What would anyone want her for?

"Unlikely. Bex is far more powerful than I am. I can barely turn the kettle on with magic."

"But you could lock a door?"

"It might not have actually been locked. I'm not sure."

"Interesting," he said, smiling suggestively. He was probably having flashbacks to their earlier activities, much like she was. It was almost tempting to forget about the Skyler issue and initiate something else between them to distract him. Hell, it would distract her.

"What's happening?" she asked, tears welling up in her eyes as she considered the various answers to the question. Something was definitely off about the Skyler situation, but she couldn't put her finger on what.

"Maybe he saw you with your familiar, or out picking cabbage leaves under the full moon or something." He shrugged.

"I don't think cabbage leaves would get you very far," she quipped, trying not to let the stress overtake her or else she'd never recover, and she couldn't return to Bex's wedding clearly upset, it would raise too many questions, especially when her Mum had just been introduced to Felix and correctly guessed that he was her mate. Eurgh, she hated that word. But there wasn't another one that was widely used by witches, and she knew even less about dryad mating habits. She guessed she'd find out later.

"Well I know next to nothing about potions. Maybe you can teach me." He nuzzled his lips into her hair, distracting the pair of them again.

"Stop," she said, pushing him away firmly. He looked hurt, but he obeyed, taking a step back and putting some much needed distance between the two of them. "We need to figure this out, Felix. If there's something dodgy going on, then I want him away from my family. Bex has enough to deal with today as it is, and don't get me started on Faye."

"Faye and the dark haired guy she was with?"

"Reese. Yes. I'll explain later." Maybe she could even enlist his help in trying to figure out the best way to help Faye and Reese move past the not being able to touch thing. Dryads were renowned for their work with natural remedies.

"Okay. Have you considered that he might have had you under some kind of enchantment?"

"Like what? A love potion?" she threw back, only for the two of them to stand in complete silence as her words sunk in. The way she'd been acting was almost exactly like someone had been using a love potion on her. "That rat bastard," she muttered.

"Meeting me must have broken through it," Felix said softly and she looked up at him, meeting his eyes and seeing the pain and hope that was there.

"Thank you," she whispered, her voice cracking as tears threatened. He smoothed his thumb over her cheek again.

"You're welcome. But don't worry, we'll figure it out."

As little as he wanted to, Felix knew that he had to go and find Robert. With his growing obsession over one of the bridesmaids, he'd almost completely abandoned his role as the best man. Not that much needed doing. Unless making sure that Robert hadn't gotten too drunk that he couldn't stand anymore. There was always a chance that could have happened.

He exited the reception room and made his way outside, something telling him that his friend would be about. If he was honest, he quite wanted to be outside and close to nature as it was. It'd been a hectic day, and being inside so much, not to mention away from his tether overnight, had taken it's toll on him. No dryad should be away from nature for that long. He couldn't regret it though, not when it was the exact turn of events that had led him to Mia. Felix smiled to himself. Despite the worrying turn of the day, and the concerns he still had about Bex and Robert's marriage, it had been a good one. Which was definitely a good thing considering this was the day he'd be telling his future children about when they asked how he met their mother.

He spotted a lone figure sat under a tree, and started to make his way over. He'd bet most of what he owned that it was Robert under the tree, though he had no clue what he was doing. Normally, Robert would be busy drinking or hitting on someone. Though the latter was probably a little difficult at his own wedding.

"Robert?" he called out, and the figure looked up, proving Felix right. He quickened his pace and soon found himself stood under the tree with his friend next to him looking a lot worse for wear. In fact, it almost looked as if Robert had been crying. Which was odd to say the least.

"What are you doing here Felix?" he slurred his words, at least Felix had got the drunk part right.

"Come to find you, it is your wedding day after all."

"Huh. Some day that turned out to be," Robert muttered, turning Felix's curiosity up a notch. Something was going on, and he suspected it was bigger than he'd originally suspected.

"What do you mean?"

"Nothing." Robert spoke quickly, waving a dismissive hand as he did.

"No, not nothing Robert. It's your wedding day, you should be inside celebrating with your *wife*." To Felix's surprise, the last word came out as a hiss, and he had to wonder what had happened to him. He didn't think that he'd ever spoken to Robert that way before. Maybe he was just on edge with the whole Skyler thing.

A rustle sounded from some bushes that were off to the side and Robert glanced around uneasily, peeking Felix's interest even more. Something was definitely off with his friend.

"You need to go Felix," Robert said, his frantic tone betraying far more than his words.

"What?"

"Go, now, don't let him see you." Well that was odd. But Felix listened, backing away slowly and going a few feet before realising that if he hung around a bit more, then maybe he could find out more about what was going. He crept up to another nearby tree, suddenly very thankful to the gardeners who'd designed the garden all those decades ago. Pulling on one of his dryad powers, he merged into the tree. Well, not merged, more like camouflaged. He was still a separate entity to the tree, but anyone looking his way would be clueless to the fact he was there. Except perhaps Mia. She'd probably be able to see him, or at the very least feel he was there. He strained his ears, wishing that he had some shifter blood, that would make this far easier he was sure.

"I don't know what you want Skyler." Robert's voice shook, which was probably to do with the other man, even Felix was a little wary of Skyler. But how did they know each other? And what was Skyler doing here?

"I want proof. That's the whole point of you being here isn't it?"

"Proof of w-what though?" Robert stuttered. If Felix hadn't been worried before, then he certainly was now.

"I want proof of Rebecca's powers. Or if not hers, Amelia's or Faye's. That family is hiding something and I want to know what it is." Skyler's voice was cold, and Felix hated the way he said Mia's full name. Almost like he held her in contempt. Things were not looking good, they were not looking good at all.

"Powers? What are you on about?" Robert sounded a bit stronger this time. Meaning that Robert was clueless about Bex's true nature. He didn't know whether that was a good thing or a bad thing.

"Anything unusual, potions, foresight, *magic*." Skyler's tone curled in contempt around the last word, which just made the whole thing even more curious. What the hell was going on with Skyler?

"Are you suggesting that Bex is a-"

"A witch. I'm not suggesting it. I'm aware of it. I just need proof. Which is where you come in." Dread found itself a spot in Felix's stomach, this wasn't good for Mia. And he needed to protect Mia at every opportunity.

"Me?" Robert squeaked, and if he'd said more, then Felix imagined that his stutter would have returned. This was nothing like the brash, confident friend that he'd come to know and kind of hate. This was a broken man.

"Yes. You're married to Rebecca now. You have a reason to be in every aspect of her life. Find me something."

"But Bex has done nothing wrong," Robert protested.

"Yet she's the reason we have your daughter."

Felix could imagine Skyler's sadistic grin as he said the words and his heart sank. He hadn't even realised that Robert had a daughter, but he could imagine having her held over his head wasn't a good thing. Hell, when Felix had a daughter, he'd do anything to protect her. Anything.

"You want Bex in return for her?" He sounded sad.

"No, I want all of the Thornheart witches for her. And you're going to get them for us."

"All?"

"Yes, all. There are six in case you're wondering." Felix frowned to himself. Three of the witches were clearly Mia and her two sisters, but who were the other three? And what was Thornheart? he'd have to ask Mia later. In a way that didn't freak her out about the fact someone seemed to be out to get her. No challenge there at all.

"Or what, you'll kill me?" Robert sounded a bit stronger this time.

"No Robert. If you don't get them, we'll kill your daughter. In front of you. Slowly." Skyler laughed, a hollow sound that had Felix convinced he was finding some kind of sadistic pleasure from this.

"Okay, I'll get them for you," Robert said, his

voice cracking with unvoiced emotion. Something needed doing to stop this. Robert might not be a good person all of the time, but even he deserved a chance to be happy, and a chance to know his daughter.

13

"WHY'VE you brought me here Mia?" Bex asked, her misery tainting her words and increasing the guilt Mia felt over not working harder to convince her not to get married. She'd cocked up massively, but had been too engrossed in Skyler to do much more. She shivered, thinking about her and Felix's realisation that she'd probably been under a love potion the entire time. There was an irony there, she was sure, but there was nothing she could do about it now.

"I thought you'd want these." Mia held out the two necklace boxes that Felix had got for her earlier. To her surprise, Bex shook her head.

"I don't want them."

"But-"

"I don't want them, Mia. Give them to Faye and see if one will open for her and Reese."

"It won't," Faye said as she walked into the small room off the side of the great hall. Mia gave her younger sister a questioning look, to which she waved a dismissive hand. "Please, the two of you disappear, I'm going to follow. You should know that by now." Mia had to admit that she had a point. It was what she'd been doing since they were children after all.

"But you were so upset about it not opening earlier," Mia said.

"I wasn't upset about that," Bex bit back. Faye placed a comforting hand on her arm, but didn't say anything. Neither did Mia. It wasn't the time right now. "I was upset because it *did* open for you. I knew it wouldn't open for me."

"How-"

"Reagan told me." Mia's mouth fell open. She'd never really considered that Reagan might have talked to Bex about this kind of thing. "And she said that I had to marry Robert if I stood any chance of saving us."

"Saving us, Bex?" Faye asked softly.

"I don't know any more, that's all Rea would say.

But there's something about a Coven and our grand-mothers, but she hasn't seen more. I'm sure you've heard what the sight is like." Mia nodded. The sight was a touchy subject for witches. Only some of them had it, and Reagan was one of the lucky few. Even her brother didn't seem to share the power, but according to his mate, his gut feelings were to be listened to under all circumstances. She liked that about Eira. She was laid back and forthcoming, even if she was asked about the fact that she had three mates. It sounded like fun to Mia, but also like a lot of hard work.

"So what do we do?" Mia asked,wondering what they could actually do with the information. Maybe they needed to talk to Reagan again, Mia was sure she'd seen her around here somewhere.

"I don't know." Bex seemed shaken, and Faye dropped her touch so that she could put her arm around Bex's shoulder.

"There's more isn't there?" she asked as she watched Faye offer comfort to their older sister. Something wasn't adding up, and she wasn't sure what it was, but she had an inkling. "How do you know none of the boxes will open for you?" Bex looked up from where she'd nestled into Faye's shoulder.

"Because I'm marrying him to save his daughter." Mia's mouth dropped open as the words sunk in.

"What?" Faye asked, pulling away to look at Bex, who now had silent tears streaming down her face.

"Robert's daughter was in trouble, and one of the ways to save her was for me to marry him."

"And you believed him?" Mia's anger was rising at the thought of her kind hearted sister being taken in by Robert's plan.

"I didn't need to, I saw a photo. They're keeping her in a cell, Mia. A fucking cell." Mia just stood there, unsure how to process what her sister was telling her.

"What can we do?" she asked softly, with Faye nodding along.

"I don't know. Robert didn't tell me what they wanted, other than him marrying me."

"Them?" Faye asked, stroking Bex's back. Mia glanced at the door, almost wanting to go and find Felix. He'd know what to do. Eurgh, when did she become that person? She wasn't the kind that needed a man around for everything to be okay.

"If you want to go find him you can," Bex said, her glazed eyes meeting Mia's. She shook her head. No way was she leaving her sisters right now.

"I don't think Robert will tell us anything we don't already know," Faye said.

"She doesn't mean Robert," Mia replied, keeping her voice soft and reassuring. "She means Felix. But I don't know where he is right now."

"Can he help?"

"I'm not sure," Mia admitted. "I can't say I know much about him apart from that he's mine."

"He's definitely it?" Bex asked, a bit of awe filling her voice. Mia nodded.

"Yes." She smiled to herself. thinking back to the fun the two of them had had in the cupboard. Yes, Felix was definitely it for her. The sparks had been more than enough to convince her of that.

"You have a smile on your face like you just got laid," Faye teased. Mia bit her lip, avoiding her sister's eyes. "Oh my God, you have. At the reception Mia? Really?"

"You understand-"

"No, Mia I don't. I can't touch my mate, remember?"

"Sorry," Mia muttered.

"No, I'm sorry, I shouldn't have snapped. Whatever the problem is between Reese and me, it's not your fault. Maybe I broke something in him that time I turned him into a toad."

"I don't think that's it, Faye," Bex interrupted for the first time.

"Then what is?"

"Remember what Reagan told us about Josh and Eira?" The two of them nodded. "Maybe it's something similar to that."

"You think we might be waiting for someone else?" Faye asked, hope blooming in her eyes.

"Maybe. It's possible."

"Don't give up Faye, you never know what might happen." Mia finally moved over to her sisters, taking each of their hands in hers. "But we have bigger things that we need to sort out. Like what the hell we're going to do about Robert."

"And about your date." Felix's voice came from the doorway and Mia instantly dropped their hands to turn to him. She wasn't even fully aware what she was doing until she was by his side and slipping an arm around his waist. Luckily, he responded instantly, putting an arm around her shoulders and dropping a soft kiss against her head. She glanced over at her sisters and saw the sad smile on Bex's face, which almost made her feel bad about how she was being with Felix. She opened her mouth to speak, but Bex held up a hand to silence her.

"Don't. My turn will come. Who am I to deny you

what we all want." Her smile spread a little more, becoming more genuine. Mia relaxed a little more into Felix who squeezed her closer.

"What do you mean what we need to do about Mia's date?" Faye asked, looking Felix up and down as she did. Probably sizing him up. "And what are you?"

"Faye, don't be rude," Bex admonished, finally slipping back into elder sister mode and chastising Faye. Mia hid a snigger in Felix's shoulder.

"I'm a dryad."

"You didn't have to tell her," Bex said, and Mia felt Felix shrug from her position tucked into him.

"Makes no difference to me. I'm sure that Mia would have told you."

"See," Faye said, and Mia could imagine her sticking her tongue out in response. Though she imagined Faye had just about held back. Mia untucked herself, there was no way she could stay hidden inside Felix's arm when there was a potential mess of her making about.

"Now what about Skyler?" she asked Felix, looking up into his concerned looking eyes.

"Who *is* Skyler?" Bex whispered to Faye.

"Her date I think. You know the blond man she's been ignoring the entire night?" Bex nodded, and

Mia threw a glare at the two of them. Though she guess it was true. She had been ignoring Skyler all night, but that was hardly her fault. She'd met her mate, that was always going to overtake any other obligation.

"Yes, Skyler's my date. Yes, I gave him a love potion," Mia said off hand. They should at least know the truth.

"You did what?" Bex sounded horrified.

"I gave him a love potion. Because for some reason I've been mooning over him for months but not actually getting anywhere."

"Except I'm pretty sure the love potion hasn't worked. When did you last give it to him?" Felix asked as he stroked her lower back soothingly.

"This morning sometime, before I went to get ready with Bex," she said having thought back over the events of the day.

"And before that?" Faye asked.

"Last night. I took a cup of coffee out to him while he was gardening."

"He was gardening?" Felix raised an eyebrow as he asked.

"Yes. Why do you think I liked him, he was in the garden almost every day...oh."

"Oh?" Bex asked.

"I think she's just realised that he was in the garden every day for just this reason," Felix answered.

"So he's known that I like the outdoors since the beginning?" Mia asked softly, worried about what that meant. Her affinity for potions, and the natural ingredients that created them, had meant that Mia had always loved being outside, though not the actual getting dirty that gardening entailed. She glanced up at Felix, she guessed it made sense that she liked the outside if fate had always had a dryad in mind for her.

"I suspect so," Felix said. "And I don't think you love potion worked."

"But Mia's potions always work. She's always been the best at them." Faye looked confused, and Mia offered her a weak smile.

"I think there's more at work here. I overheard Robert talking to Skyler."

"Oh no." Bex's eyes widened and the blood rushed from her face. Mia watched in amazement as her mate and her sister held each other's gaze, something important passing between them.

"You know don't you?"

She nodded slowly. "I suspected."

"And you married him anyway?" Felix asked.

"There is a child on the line." Bex rose to her feet, her spine ramrod straight and fury burning behind her eyes. She closed the short gap between her and Felix and poked a finger to his chest. "Do you think I would marry someone who wasn't my one without a good reason? A little girl has been kidnapped. I have seen the pictures. He told me that if I married him, then he'd be able to save her. So I did. Robert is my friend, I wanted to help."

"Your friend?" Mia was relieved that Faye had asked, she didn't particularly want to get between Bex and Felix, that was one way to have her loyalty ripped in two.

"Yes, I've known Robert for years. There's nothing between us but friendship, at the altar is the first time we've kissed since we got drunk four years ago." Well that was surprising. And no wonder the few times they'd actually tried to change Bex's mind she'd resisted. She was doing this out of a sense of decency and not because she wanted to actually be with Robert.

"Which bring us back to what are we going to do now?" Mia asked, breaking the tension between Felix and Bex as they squared off.

"I don't know." Bex deflated slightly and Faye rushed forward to support her. Something definitely wasn't right with her sister. Maybe it was just the stress that had got to her, and a few nights decent sleep would do her good.

"All we have to do is deal with Skyler, while keeping Robert's daughter safe, right?" Mia asked, feeling uneasy already. There was a life at risk, and that wasn't something to be messed with. Nor was it something Mia particularly wanted on her shoulders. But Bex had clearly been distressed by what she'd seen, and Mia would support her whatever she decided.

14

Felix hated feeling nervous. He tried to avoid situations that scared him, and this was definitely one of those. He hated that there was a little girl's life at risk, and he hated that Mia was going to put herself in harm's way to try and stop that. Especially as what he'd overheard earlier implied that it wasn't just Mia that would satisfy the witch hunter. He wanted more of her coven. Though the sisters had told him that they didn't actually have one. No one in their family had since their Grandma, who they all smiled about whenever they mentioned. It was sweet to see. They'd clearly been close to her.

"Are you sure about this?" he asked, tucking a strand of dark hair behind Mia's ear and looking deep into her eyes.

"What other choice do I have?" she replied, a resigned look on her face. Yes, that was about right. There was no other choice and they just had to kind of get on with it. Didn't mean that he felt any better about her being in danger.

"I suppose we don't. I just hate the idea of you being alone with him."

"Why? Nothing's going to happen Felix. I might have thought I loved him, but that was probably just a potion talking, you know that." He did. It was seeming more and more likely that she'd been under a love potion the entire time she'd been lusting after Skyler. Especially with how quickly things had switched today. Though he guessed there was a possibility that it was meeting him that had made the difference. Whatever it was, he didn't really care. So long as she was safe. So long as she was his.

"It's not what could happen between you that worries me, it's what he could do *to* you."

"I'll be fine, Felix. I know my magic isn't the strongest, but it *will* protect me if it needs to. That's how it works."

"Are you sure?" She bit her bottom lip, a sure indication that she wasn't as convinced as she was trying to pretend she was, but he let it slide. He didn't want to dent her confidence just before she went to face Skyler. She'd need all her wits about her.

"What if he tries to drug me again?"

"I don't think he will. But if he does, it probably won't work right?"

"I don't know. I'm flying a bit blind here. A properly brewed love potion should always work, unless there's true mates involved..." she looked away, breaking their gaze. Felix placed two gentle fingers under her chin and tilted her face up so that their eyes locked again.

"If you're doubting that this is the real thing, then you can stop. But if you want proof..." He imagined that his eyes sparkled with mischief as he closed the short distance between them and pressed his lips to hers. Sparks began to ignite behind his eyes, but this time, he was pretty sure they were just in his head and not caused by the two of them connecting. She pushed her body against his, and the warm supple feel of it was enough to almost have him forgetting about all their responsibilities and taking her right there. He had to wonder if he'd ever get enough of her. He hoped not.

They broke apart, both breathing heavily, and he regretted not being able to spend more time with her before sending her off to face someone who was probably out to kill her. Not a pleasant thought.

"I have to go," she whispered, touching her fingers to her lips. He nodded, unable to speak through the lump in his throat. She gave him a weak smile, before turning and walking through the door, away from him and towards danger. The instant she was gone, the curtain they'd been stood behind whipped back, revealing Faye and Bex watching him with determined looks on their faces.

"She's stronger than she looks you know," Faye said, while Bex nodded beside her.

"I've no doubt of that, it's just hard to let her go into danger without me. Do you like watching your mate leave?" he asked her. Faye shook her head, tears glistening in her eyes and Felix wondered if he'd hit on a nerve, remembering the strained glances and movements between Faye and the man she was at the wedding with.

"She'll do what needs to be done. Maybe then we'll have some more answers." Bex straightened her spine, looking more like the woman he thought he knew rather than the withdrawn one he'd witnessed today. But at least that all made sense now. She wasn't marrying Robert because of some misguided idea that she could change him or anything, which made Felix feel a little better in his role of letting the wedding go ahead. As selfish as that was.

"So what do we do with ourselves while we wait for Mia to get back?" he asked, hoping the sisters had something that would take his mind off the woman he wanted to keep safe more than he wanted anything. Even life itself. Damn, he hoped being mated wasn't going to make him think in clichés all the time, that would truly suck.

15

MIA STRAIGHTENED HER SPINE, steeling herself for the confrontation that was about to come. The others had suggested that she pretended not to know anything, but she wasn't convinced that that was even possible anymore, not when she knew the depths to which Skyler had sunk. And she wasn't thinking about the love potion when she thought that either. She might not have known that Robert even had a daughter, but she wasn't the kind of woman to sit back and let it slide once she knew.

She scanned the dance floor, trying to bleach the sight of her Dad doing the Cha-Cha Slide out of her mind. That should be her though, having a good time with her sisters and dancing to cheesy pop music, but she guessed that would have to wait.

Maybe when she got married to Felix, they could have a wedding that would go down without anyone trying to kidnap and murder people. Hell, Skyler wasn't even trying on the kidnapping part, he'd downright done it. And if what Felix had heard was correct, Mia was going to be his next victim, with Bex and Faye to follow. Which was stupid to say the least. Anyone that knew her knew not to mess with her family. It was the quickest way to get on her bad side, and that was somewhere that no one ever wanted to be.

She spotted him leaning against the bar, a glass of something clear clutched in his hand. Probably water. If she was planning to kidnap someone then she certainly wouldn't be drinking. Sure, she could make it so that the alcohol didn't affect her in theory, but she wouldn't want to test that on such an important occasion. She snorted to herself, why the hell was she thinking about how she would kidnap someone? What weird turn of events had led to here? She waved at Skyler and plastered a fake smile on her face. He'd probably figured out that his love potion had worn off, but she didn't want to let him know for sure, especially if it wasn't actually a love potion and was some kind of other enchantment instead. But then, where could he have got it from? She'd never got any paranormal vibes off him before, though admittedly, she'd been too distracted to truly be looking before. Well now she just felt bad for using her own on him. Sure, he turned out to be a bad guy, but it was still a horrible feeling knowing that it would make him so unaware of his normal behaviours.

She weaved her way through the guests, making a beeline for the man at the end of the bar, who was now waving to one of the bar staff.

"Hi," she said, trying to infuse her voice with a note of breathlessness. It was helping to picture that she was talking to Felix, but even she could see through her fakeness.

"Hey, beautiful." Skyler smiled, and Mia felt sick to her stomach as an uneasy feeling overtook her. Skyler took a glass from the barman and handed it to her, leaving her no choice but to take it. He watched on as Mia brought the glass to her lips and took a small sip of the cold tart wine. It slid down her throat easily. Unfortunately it was swiftly followed by the an odd feeling like something was sliding down her skin, only adding to her general unease. Was this what a love potion felt like when it took effect? She started to shudder, but caught herself just in time and plastered what she hoped was a lovesick smile on her face.

"Where've you been? I've been looking every-where for you?" she asked, slipping a hand onto his chest. His muscles were as hard as Felix's were, but they held none of the warmth that the dryad's did. She didn't like that. It felt wrong. In fact, the instinct to pull her hand away from him and break the touch completely was almost too much to ignore. She took a deep breath. She had to do this. There was too much at stake for her not to do this.

"I've been looking for you. I even checked the cleaning cupboards, but there was nothing there." Ice formed in Mia's veins as his words sunk in. So he knew about the cupboard, or maybe he was just guessing about it. But then, if he knew about that, did he know about Felix? And if he knew about Felix, then did he know that his love potion wasn't working on her. "Got you." He said his smile turning from a fakely affectionate one, to something far more predatory. Mia gulped. This wasn't good at all.

"W-what do you mean, got me?" she asked, giving up all pretence of pretending to be under the spell. There was just no point anymore.

"What are you Amelia?"

"I don't know what you mean." She shook her

head and tried to take a step back, but Skyler's hand closed down on her wrist, holding her steady and close to him.

"I think you do. So answer me this, Amelia Thornheart, what are you? And how did you stop the potion working?"

"How did you?" she threw back, finding her strength again as her magic responded to the perceived threat. She could feel it simmering just below the surface, and knew that if she let it, it could cause an almighty stir. She may not be that naturally talented of a witch, but magic never failed when it's owner was in danger. It was the same with shifters. They had a tendency of shifting automatically when danger was near, a trait a lot of them still struggled to tamp down on when they were out and about in the human world.

Thing was, could she risk her magic exploding here? She was in a room with a lot of humans, how would they take blue sparks flying from her skin and causing damage she couldn't even imagine? Not well probably. Then they'd possibly have more than just Skyler to deal with. Mia glanced over her shoulder, hoping to see her sisters and Felix, or maybe even her Dad, he'd know that something was wrong after just a glance. But no one seemed to be paying any attention to the couple in the corner. Probably believing that they were just having a moment between them.

"That's none of your business really, Amelia. Now are you going to come with me quietly, or am I going to have to make you?" The creepy grin accompanying his words gave her little doubt that he could, and would, make her if he needed to, but she really didn't want to make a scene. Skyler no longer seemed the type to just let any witnesses be. And she had to protect the other people in the room. She didn't want anyone else in danger because of her.

"I'll come quietly," she said, whispering the words as if hoping that he wouldn't hear them and wouldn't actually take her up on them.

16

"SOMETHING'S WRONG." He didn't know what, but Felix's gut was telling him it was true, and he didn't want to think about what that meant. In fact, it probably could only mean that Mia was in danger, and whatever happened, he couldn't just stand by while that was the case. Not when he'd just found her.

"It's probably nothing," Bex said, as she paced back and forth in the room. A rapid pounding on the door made all three of them jump. Faye was the first to recover and she pushed to her feet to open it. Felix's heart was in his throat, the rhythmic pounding almost reassuring, but not quite. He hoped it was Mia on the other side. She might knock if she thought they wouldn't just let anyone in. Really, they should have thought about that before they let her go. Otherwise a situation like this one could happen.

Faye swung open the door, revealing a redhead who he vaguely recognised, though that was probably just because she was another wedding guest, he'd work it out later when he could focus his thoughts on something that wasn't Mia and the potential danger she was in.

"Reagan?" Bex asked. "Is everything okay?"

"Tell me Mia's here," Reagan responded, her eyes looking wildly around the room and taking in the three of them and their on edge stances. "She's not, is she?" Felix shook his head when neither of the other two answered. A worried look flew over the new woman's face, which didn't do anything to help Felix's anxiety levels.

"What do you know?"

"Nothing, I just had a feeling that I needed to check where Mia was." She sounded frantic, as if there really was something to be concerned about. And yet, she didn't question who he was at all.

"I'm-"

"Felix, yes I know." She waved away his outstretched hand as she cut him off, and Felix frowned at her.

"Because I'm the best man?"

"No, because you're Mia's mate and I see things."
She walked over to wear Bex was standing and put
her hands on the other woman's cheeks before
starting to whisper something that Felix couldn't
hear. Instead of doing anything about that, he just
frowned. What an odd way of acting.

"She has the sight," Faye supplied. as she came to
stand beside him.

"A witch thing?"

"Yes, have you seriously not heard of it?" He
shook his head.

"There's only a handful of witches born with it,
even within families. Her brother doesn't even have
it, though I've been told not to ignore his gut feelings." Faye's bubbly tone wasn't convincing Felix in
the slightest. If anything she was more nervous than
he was. Giving in to his instincts, he pulled her to
him and hugged her tight. Not in the way that he
would hug Mia, but rather the way he'd hug his own
sister. Not that Autumn would let him hug her, she
was notoriously closed off around everyone and he
wished he knew why. Something to do with the time
she'd got lost in the woods when they were children
he was sure, but she refused to talk about it.

A sniffle at his shoulder surprised him, and Faye
bunched up a handful of his shirt. Not that it would

make any difference to how it looked, it was still scrunched from it's trip to the cleaning cupboard floor when he and Mia had slept together. With difficulty, he brought his thoughts back around to the present. Thinking about sex with his mate, while comforting her sister, was weird in anyone's book.

"I'm sorry." Faye pulled away, trailing a hand under her eyes and wiping away the stray tears that had collected there. "I'm not used to being held anymore."

"Why?" he whispered, vaguely aware that Bex and Reagan had stopped their own whispering in order to pay attention to his and Faye's exchange. He didn't take his eyes off Faye's though, he didn't want her freaking out by thinking that her sister was listening, even if she was.

"I can't touch my mate. I don't want anyone else to touch me, so it kind of leaves me lonely."

"Oh Faye," Bex said, rushing forward and pulling her youngest sister towards her, wrapping her up in her arms. "Why didn't you tell me?"

"You had your own things going on. You were with Robert, and planning the wedding, and really it's not new that I can't touch Reese. We're kind of used to it by now."

"That doesn't mean that you needed to have gone

through that alone. We would have been there for you the moment you needed us." Bex smoothed a hand along Faye's back and the blonde woman let out a sob before regaining her composure.

"Can we talk about this later?" she asked, sniffing. "Let's figure out where Mia's got to first." The worry in the pit of Felix's stomach took hold again now that the focus was back on his mate.

"We need to find her," he said, a finality in his tone that really couldn't be denied. Or it could be, but it wouldn't end very well for anyone that tried. Which surprised him, he wasn't normally so bloody minded, but this time he was.

"I agree. Something is really not right," Reagan added.

"I thought you said I'd stop this by marrying Robert?" Bex probably should have sounded angry at that, but she didn't. Instead, it just sounded like she was sad.

"I think it will help, I just don't know how," Reagan tried to explain. "But for now, I think I need to follow Felix." All three women looked at him, and he was suddenly rather self-conscious about himself.

"Why me?" he whispered.

"You're her mate, you feel a bond right?" He

nodded. He wasn't quite sure what he felt was a bond, but there was definitely something, and he was pretty sure it connected him to Mia.

"I can follow it?"

"You should be able to," Reagan answered. "Just focus inwards on it and let instinct do the rest." He did what she suggested, and honed in on a slightly glowing centre within himself. To his surprise, he found a pale blue ball of sparks marking up a lattice of willow leaves. Outwardly, he smiled. He supposed that was the perfect combination of him and Mia. It made sense that that was what their bond looked like. Guess there was no doubt that they were truly meant to be.

17

MIA TRIED to kick Skyler in the shins but struggled. While she may have agreed to go with him, she hadn't expected for him to grab her around the waist and all but hoist her over his shoulder, it was a wonder that no one had noticed him doing it. Then again, there were other things about him that made her think that he had some kind of magic of his own, or at least access to someone that did. It probably wasn't too difficult to have someone else making potions for him, but the other stuff seemed little more implausible. Yet he gave off no sense of magic, and she'd certainly not seen anything that looked like him using it.

"Let me go, Skyler." She tried to draw on her

magic, but something was blocking it, confusing her all the more. No one had the power to do that as far as she knew. Not even necromancers, and their magic worked differently than witches and other paranormals, something to do with the life and death magic, she didn't really understand if she was honest.

"You said you'd come with me, Amelia." Eurgh, she hated that he was using her full name. Why was he doing that? She hardly ever used it herself, her friends definitely called her Mia, as did her family unless she was in trouble.

"Where are you even taking me?" She was still trying to kick his shins, and started wriggling around in order to try and loosen his grip too. Not that it was working, he was surprisingly strong.

"Nowhere that concerns you." She shivered, not liking the sound of that at all, and began chanting Felix's name in her head. She knew it wouldn't do anything. Not even mates could communicate tele-pathically between themselves, never mind ones that had only known each other less than twenty-four hours. Even so, the sound of his name in her head was helping her cope with the situation, and giving her a little bit more strength to carry on. Not that it was doing anything to solve the magic issue. She still couldn't access it, which was increasing her worry by the second.

He bundled her into the trunk of a car, her arms and legs scrunching up in the small space, and she struggled against him more, failing miserably as her magic refused to come yet again. Without it, there was no way that she could fight against his larger size and strength. As the trunk slammed shut, leaving her with a lingering view of Skyler's sadistic grin branded in her head, Mia tried to avoid the panic that was about to set in. She couldn't let it. If she did, then she was as good as dead. Or drained. Or whatever the hell else Sklyer wanted with her. At this rate, he'd be tying her to a stake and preparing to burn her. Well that was a cheery thought. Mia scolded herself, hating that she was having such dark musings. A tear began to slide down her face as she considered her sisters, and Felix, who'd she'd left behind. What if she never saw them again? No. She wasn't going to go there. She *couldn't* go there. No way was she one of those people who found and lost their mate within a day. She refused to be that helpless.

She breathed in and out slowly, trying to regain

her composure. Mia was not a damsel in distress. It wasn't a role that suited her in the slightest. The car started to move, the low rumbling of the engine vibrating through Mia. She crossed her fingers and hoped that he wouldn't go far. She'd heard that mates could follow the bond between them, but didn't know how far that bond would stretch. And she definitely didn't want to test it. She'd just have to hope Felix wasn't far behind. If he even knew that she was in trouble. *No. Stop it*. She couldn't think like that if she was going to get through this.

The journey seemed to last forever, but it was probably only a matter of ten minutes, probably even less. She had no way of telling without her phone, which was abandoned in the clutch bag she'd left somewhere at the reception along with her Grandma's necklaces. Horror filled her as she realised that she hadn't put hers on yet. And now that she was sure that it had something to do with meeting her mate, she really wanted to be wearing it, she thought that it might make her feel closer to Felix and the bond that the two of them already shared. Well, hopefully already shared. Weird how she'd gone from not recognising what was between them, to wanting the bond to be real enough that she could touch it.

At a complete loss for what else to do, Mia focused inwards, trying to centre herself on the place that her magic lived, or at the very least where she imagined it lived. It was all very complex and, for some reason that completely baffled her, witches just didn't talk about their magic. Just like they didn't talk about their familiars, the loss of which was really stinging Mia at the moment. She was alone, and she was in trouble, Squeak should be here and yet he wasn't. A sure sign that something was very very wrong.

The trunk of the car opened, letting the cold night air surround Mia and chilling her to the bone. She shivered, and it was enough to distract her as Skyler hoisted her into his arms. Once she was there, she began to struggle again, but like before, Skyler had to upper body strength not to be fazed by it. Though she did wonder where he got it from. Maybe he wasn't as human as she thought.

He carried her through the corrugated iron door that led into what looked like a warehouse. A warehouse that looked worryingly like the ones that always seemed to show up in horror movies whenever someone was kidnapped. Great, she was going to end up murdered in a warehouse on the day of her sister's fake wedding. Not the end that she'd ever had in mind.

The interior was dim, lit only by a few waning light bulbs that seemed not to be getting enough electricity to actually be making any light. All it did was add to the ominous feel of the place. She really hoped that Felix came soon. Or that her magic returned. Either of those possibilities would make her feel less alone and more like she could get out of this alive.

From her position in Skyler's arms, she could make out desks, and even what looked like an operating table, not a good sign. He turned left, his footsteps echoing in the otherwise silent warehouse. *Don't panic.* Panicking would get no one anywhere.

One of Skyler's arms loosened, and she considered making a break for it, but not knowing where she was, and wearing a bridesmaid dress and high heels, she didn't imagine that she'd get very far. It was better to wait for a more convenient moment to make her escape. Plus, if she was where she thought she was, then she might be able to find out what had happened to Robert's daughter.

With his spare hand, Skyler opened a solid looking metal door, much like the ones that Mia saw on TV whenever a character was unlucky enough to end up visiting prison. He threw her into the room, and he sprawled to the floor, scraping her knees as she did, a sharp ripping sound letting her know that her dress was also ruined. It was a shame, but she guessed that tonight wouldn't be one she wanted to remember anyway.

"I'll be seeing you tomorrow, Amelia. Sleep well." His voice was cold, chilling her even more. He slammed the metal door slammed shut behind him, leaving her alone in the gloom.

Or at least she thought she was alone. Mia looked up slowly and her eyes met the wide brown ones of a frightened child. Guess she'd just discovered what they'd done with Robert's daughter. She scrambled to her feet, kicking off her heels, she didn't need them here anyway, and made her way slowly towards the frightened little girl. She crouched down slowly and looked into her eyes, holding out her hands to show that she wasn't anyone to be scared of.

"Hi, I'm Mia," she said softly, trying not to spook her. "What's your name?"

"Fiona," the little girl said.

"I'm here to keep you safe now, Fiona, is that

okay?" The little girl nodded her head, and Mia held out her arms. Without a second thought, Fiona buried into them, and Mia closed her arms around her. They'd made a grave mistake in putting her in the same room as the child; now she had even more reason to get free.

18

FELIX SLAMMED on the breaks of the car as he passed a small dirt track off to the left. He wasn't sure what it was that made him certain he needed to turn down it, but now wasn't the time to question that. Now was the time to act first, then think about it later and hope to God that he got to Mia before anything too bad happened. Whatever too bad might be.

A warehouse loomed up ahead and he brought the car to an abrupt stop, causing Faye to press her hands against the dashboard in an attempt to keep herself steady.

"You need to calm down," she said through gritted teeth.

"Would you be any different if Reese was in trouble?" he threw back, the silence on her part being enough to tell him that she knew he was telling the truth. She'd be exactly the same, if not worse because their bond had had longer to form itself, even if they couldn't touch.

He opened his door, and jumped from the car, vaguely aware that Faye was doing the same on her side. It was just the two of them, Bex and Reagan had stayed at the wedding to hold down the fort, and to try and extract Robert from whatever trouble he'd managed to get himself into. Felix had tried to get Faye to stay too, not wanting to put her in danger, but she'd soon pointed out that he had no combative powers of his own, and would probably need a witch with him if he stood a chance of getting Mia back.

"Fancy giving us a light?" he asked. He didn't mind the dark, but this was kind of eerie, and he hated the thought of Mia being here, especially if she was alone. He was freaked out enough, and he hadn't been carted off by a crazy witch hunter.

"I can't." She sounded as if she was almost in pain, and he glanced back at her to dimly make out the shape of her clicking her fingers.

"Why not?"

"I don't know, something's blocking me." Her attention wavered from her fingers, and her eyes met Felix's. Even in the dark he could see them widen, as if she'd had the same thought that he had. If Faye couldn't use her magic, then Mia wouldn't be able to use hers either. And if she couldn't, then chances were she had no way of defending herself. He knew full well that she didn't have any weapons stashed under her bridesmaid's dress, and he doubted that Faye did either.

In the same instant, they broke eye contact and began running towards the warehouse.

19

SOMETHING WAS ABOUT TO CHANGE, and she didn't quite know what. But the tingle in the air, and at her fingertips, had her pushing Fiona behind her in a weak attempt to protect her. It likely wouldn't do much if it was Sklyer coming, and it definitely wouldn't if he wasn't alone. But she had to at least try. If not, then she'd blame herself for as long as she lived. Not that she was going to live long if where she was now was any indication. The medical tables worried her, especially the fact that they were out in the open and not closed off by curtains like they would be in a hospital. She shivered. Hopefully whatever was blocking her magic would fail and she'd be able to use it again. Maybe then she'd stand a chance of saving herself and Fiona. Though maybe not. Her magic was hardly worthy of the name after all.

"What's happening?" The little girl's voice shook, sounding even more panicked because of the childish lisp that she seemed to have. If Mia had to guess, she'd probably say Fiona was four or five, but she'd never really had much to do with children before, so had no way of knowing. But however old she was, she was still too young to be away from her parents. Or to have seen the horrors that she clearly had by being locked in a cell.

Anger bubbled up inside Mia, building up in a way that wasn't completely dissimilar than how it had with Felix earlier. Except that this wasn't fuelled by desire. This was fuelled by the knowledge that Skyler not only wasn't what he seemed, but that he also didn't have any sense of human decency. He couldn't have if this was what he did to a child.

She glanced down and noticed a lone blue spark leaping off one of her fingers. Now that was more like it. She focused on her magic, and more sparks joined the first, her hands now almost dancing with them. She didn't think she'd ever felt this powerful before. Taking care that she wouldn't accidentally catch the little girl, she sent the sparks towards the door, instructing them to unlock. Not that that was what happened. Instead, the door flew off it's hinges, crashing into the wall opposite the prison she'd been kept in. If being kept there for less than a few hours actually counted as being locked in. Whatever the logistics of it, there was now an open doorway for Mia and the little girl to go through. Which might not be the best plan if there were other people waiting on the other side, but anything was better than staying here in the dark.

With her magic buzzing, Mia lit a ball of light, making the dark room glow an eerie blue. Mia shivered. If she hadn't already been unnerved then she would be now. She held her free hand out to Fiona, who took it in hers, and walked slowly towards the door. She peered each way, trying to check for anyone that might be lurking, but saw no one. It didn't surprise her much. There hadn't been anyone about when Skyler had brought her here and left again, and it hadn't been that long really.

"Mia?" the little girl asked, sounding like she was about to cry. Mia squeezed her hand, but shook her head, hoping that was enough to offer some comfort, but also the need to stay quiet. Fiona nodded her head and held a finger to her lips in an exaggerated move.

The two of them crept forward, surprisingly

quietly to say that one of them was a small child. Mia
looked around her again, trying to keep up on
whether there was anyone about to take them off
guard. Her magic seemed to be holding for the
moment, but knowing her, it could short out at any
point. It wasn't like she'd ever managed to use it for
this long before without something going wrong.

A shadow crossed the open door of the warehouse, and Mia tugged sharply on Fiona's hand,
making the little girl cry out in surprise before clap-
ping one of her pudgy hands over her mouth.

"It's okay," Mia whispered, knowing that she
needed to keep the girl quiet, and that panic over the
one sound wasn't the way to do that. "We just have to
be even quieter now. I need to turn out the light,
okay?" The little girl nodded, and with a large
amount of regret, Mia extinguished her ball of
magic, hoping that she'd be able to get it back when
she needed it. If this was a one time occurrence, then
she was going to be kicking herself later.

Mia crouched down, and gestured for the two of
them to creep from one desk to another. Maybe if
they could get to the front door, they could sneak
out around the back. She supposed that then they'd
have the problem of actually getting back to her
sister's wedding, and the even bigger problem of

explaining a dirty and withdrawn child, but she'd worry about that when the time came.

The shadow moved forward, splitting into two and dread filled Mia's stomach. No way could she take two of them, especially with her untrained magic. And even more so while she had a child to keep safe. Which meant that really she needed to confront them while Fiona wasn't close.

"Stay here," she whispered, and Fiona nodded, slipping one of her thumbs into her mouth. Damn, being around a child was making Mia kind of broody. But no way was she ready for parenthood. Though maybe now she'd met Felix it wouldn't be as far off as she first thought.

She stood up, walking as quietly as she could towards the two figures. When she was a few metres away from where Fiona was hiding, she summoned her magic again, not trying to form it into a ball this time, but instead letting the sparks crackle out like lightening, filling the room with pale blue flashes. There was a feminine squeal, which surprised her, there'd been no women around when Skyler had arrived with her.

She cracked her magic again, letting the room light up, but this time something caught her attention and didn't let go. There was a familiar sent in the air, like an autumn breeze coming in through the trees. Something about it soothed her, and her magic began to wane. Which couldn't be happening. How the hell was Mia going to get out of here if her magic failed? It wasn't as if she had any self defence skills to fall back on. Maybe she should do something about that.

"Mia?" a steady male voice called out. One that she recognised, and not as the man that she thought she'd cared for for months. Her magic dropped, and she did with it, just about managing to catch herself on one of the desks that was next to her.

"Felix?" she asked, her voice barely above a whisper. She didn't want to speak any louder in case Skyler had returned. Which just made her wonder where the hell had he got to, and more importantly, what was he up to.

"It's us." The shadow moved forward, with the second one coming to meet him. If the man was Felix, then that must mean that the woman was one of her sisters. Probably Faye, she'd be missed less than Bex would. It would certainly cause a stir if the bride disappeared from her own wedding.

"What are you doing here?"

"We came to find you," he said, taking her into his arms and pressing a kiss to her forehead. She instantly felt better, her magic sparking back to life as it came home. Odd thought maybe, but it was what it was.

"How?"

"I just followed the bond. We're the real deal, Mia." She laughed softly.

"Yeah, I kind of figured that." He leaned down and pressed his lips to hers, kissing her tenderly, but not with quite the fire he'd kissed her with earlier. That could come later. That *would* be coming later if Mia had anything to do with it.

A shuffling noise distracted Mia, and she broke away, glancing behind her to find that Fiona had come out from behind the desks. If Mia hadn't been so relieved that Felix had found her, then she'd be annoyed that the girl had put herself so at risk by leaving safety.

"Fiona?" The little girl ran up to Mia, and wrapped her hands around her legs. She dropped down so that they were eye to eye. "We can go now, somewhere safe. Then we'll get you back to your Daddy." The little shook her head.

"Don't want Daddy. Want Mummy."

"I don't know where your Mummy is," Mia said gently. "But we'll do everything that we can to find her." Fiona nodded enthusiastically, sticking her thumb back into her mouth. Mia picked her up in her arms and passed her to Felix, who took the girl without question.

"You brought a car?" He nodded. "Take her there, please."

"Okay." He ushered Faye with him, not questioning what Mia was about to do. Which was good, he might not approve if he had any idea.

Mia focused on her magic, pulling it into her and focusing on the building sensation. It wasn't angry anymore. It was more resigned. She wasn't all that sure that she wanted to do this, but really there were no other options. She might not know where Skyler was, but she couldn't let this place stand. When she'd gathered all the power she could, she unleashed it, sparks flying everywhere as it ripped the warehouse apart brick by brick, somehow avoiding the bubble surrounding Mia.

20

THE CAR RIDE back had been quiet, and the little girl that Mia had found had spent the entire ride wrapped around Felix. While he was glad that she was safe, and he assumed that she was Robert's missing daughter, that just raised a lot more questions than it answered. Like why Robert and his daughter had been singled out in the first place, and how Mia had managed to level an entire warehouse without much of a thought, especially given that she claimed not to be powerful in the slightest.

The walk up to the reception hall was dragging, and he held out his hand to Mia, who took it instantly, leaving Felix feeling rejuvenated just by touching her. He looked up to see Bex coming out of the door with Reagan in tow, a relieved look on her face. From her place on his shoulder, Fiona perked up and looked around, leaning out and doing grabby hands in Bex's direction. Which was a little odd to say the least, but he was prepared to go with it. Fiona was Robert's daughter after all, and if Bex had been pretending with him for a long time, then it was likely that they knew each other. Felix let go of Mia's hand so that he could put the little girl, and he smiled as she ran towards Bex.

"Mummy!" He glanced quickly at Mia who was looking between Fiona and Bex in rapid succession, her hand flying to her mouth.

"Fee." Bex collapsed to the floor, her princess style wedding dress ballooning around her, and she paid no attention as the little girl trampled all over it and into her arms. Both of them were had tear tracks down their faces, and seemed to be repeating one another's names over and over again.

"What?" Faye's face said it all. Almost like she couldn't believe what she was seeing. Felix couldn't either.

"You never said Bex had a daughter," he muttered quietly to Mia.

"I didn't know."

"And she said the girl that had been taken was

Robert's daughter." He frowned, something wasn't adding up.

"But she can't be." Mia looked at her sister with a peculiar expression on her face.

"Robert doesn't know," Reagan said as she reached them. "He thinks Fiona's his, but she's not."

"Why didn't Bex tell us?" Faye sounded hurt, and Felix didn't blame her. If he found out Autumn had a four year old he didn't know about then he'd be pretty hurt himself.

"Maybe she was scared," Mia whispered. "Something is going on here. Something that Skyler was a part of. Maybe Bex already knew about it."

"But we're not going to get it out of her today," Felix added softly, and the two sisters nodded their heads as Reagan smiled. He slipped his hand gently on Mia's back, drawing her away from the sobbing mother and daughter. "Let's leave them for now." Mia nodded again and turned away, only glancing behind her once to check on Bex. He was surprised she only managed the once, but then there were still a lot of unanswered questions.

21

"Mɪᴀ!" Bex called out just as Mia's hand landed on the handle of her hotel room. She turned, looking towards her sister, who was still wearing her wedding dress and with her daughter wrapped around her. Her *daughter*. That was going to take some getting used to. And some explaining. But now wasn't the time to ask Bex probing questions, enough had happened today without adding more stress into the equation.

"You okay?" she asked, grateful for Felix's steadying hand on the small of her back. He hadn't left her side since they'd returned, and while she wouldn't say it outloud, she was grateful for that.

"Thank you."

"For what?"

"For saving her." Bex's eyes glistened with unshed tears. Mia pulled away from Felix's touch and laid a gentle hand on Bex's arm.

"I'd have saved her even if she wasn't yours." Their eyes met, and Bex nodded, probably seeing the sincerity that Mia was trying to convey.

"There's something else." Bex held out a long slim box to Mia, and she sighed. She'd forgotten about the necklaces.

"But what about yours?" Mia frowned. There were a lot of unanswered questions, particularly how her sister had even had a child when she hadn't met her mate yet. And if she had met her mate, then how come the boxes didn't open for her?

"It's not mine anymore." She glanced at the little girl who was almost asleep on her shoulder and smiled at her. Mia's heart lifted. She didn't think she'd seen her sister this content in years. Definitely not the time for awkward questions.

"Thank you." She took the box, the feel of it heavy in her hand, then watched as her sister turned and walked away, singing quietly under her breath.

"Is that what I think it is?" Felix asked in her ear, having stepped up behind her once more.

"Yes," Mia whispered. He took the box from her

gently, and the sparks sprung to life over her hands again.

"Let's go inside."

"Yes," she whispered again, waving a hand towards the door and hearing the tell tale click of it unlocking. The pair of them hurried through, impatience battering away inside Mia. She knew where this was going, and it couldn't happen soon enough.

She leaned an arm around her back, reaching for the zipper of her ruined dress. "Let me," Felix said softly, replacing her hand with his own and drawing the metal slowly downwards. His skin brushed hers, and her breathing quickened. She didn't want to wait any longer, she couldn't wait any longer. Her dress fell to the floor with a slight thud, and Mia was happy to know that it could stay there this time, and she'd never have to wear the damn thing again.

She spun in Felix's arms and lifted her hands to make quick work of his tie, but instead of letting her, he took a step back.

"One thing at once," he said, smiling and holding up the jewellery box. With a slightly satisfied air, he clicked it open, revealing the slightly glowing crystal inside. He pulled the necklace from the box and gestured for Mia to turn around, which she reluctantly did. A warmth spread through her as Felix

stepped close again, pressing himself along her back
as he draped the necklace around her neck and
fastened the clasp, peppering kisses along her skin
after he did.

This time, Mia wasn't letting him get away, and
when she turned around, she pressed her lips to his,
taking him with all the passion she could muster.
Felix didn't hesitate, and between them, they made
short work of his clothes, which ended up in the
heap with hers even if the suit was salvageable.

She walked slowly backwards, refusing to lose
physical contact with Felix as she did, until her legs
hit the bed. She brought him down on top of her, the
weight reassuring. He trailed one of his hands up the
inside of her thigh, but Mia shook her head.

"No, need you, no time," she panted. Felix chuckled, the sound vibrating through her. But he also did
as she asked, guiding himself towards her. She
bucked her hips against him, desperate to feel the
full effect of the sparks that were already starting to
form along her skin. They moved together in a
rhythm that was solely their own, and one that
proved just how right they were together. And it was
in that moment that Mia knew she'd got everything
that she never knew she wanted.

Maybe giving the wrong man a love potion

wasn't the worst thing in the world after all. Not when it gave her this.

Thank you for reading *The Hunter's Potion*. If you want to read more from The Paranormal Council series, you can with *The Banshee's Spark*: https://books2read.com/thebansheesspark/

Books in the Obscure World

- Ashryn Barker Trilogy (urban fantasy, completed series)
- Grimalkin Academy: Kittens Series (paranormal academy, completed series)
- Grimalkin Academy: Catacombs Trilogy (paranormal academy, completed series)
- City Of Blood Trilogy (urban fantasy)
- Grimalkin Academy: Stakes Trilogy (paranormal academy)
- The Harpy Bounty Hunter Trilogy (urban fantasy)
- The Black Fan (vampire romance)
- Sabre Woods Academy (paranormal academy)
- Scythe Grove Academy (urban fantasy)
- Carnival Of Knives (urban fantasy)

Books in the Forgotten Gods World

- The Queen of Gods Trilogy

(paranormal/mythology romance)

- Forgotten Gods Series
(paranormal/mythology romance)

The Grimm World

- Grimm Academy Series (fairy tale academy)
- Fate Of The Crown Duology (Arthurian Academy)
- Once Upon An Academy Series (Fairy Tale Academy)

Books in the Paranormal Council Universe

- The Paranormal Council Series (shifter romance, completed series)
- The Fae Queen Of Winter Trilogy (paranormal/fantasy)
- Thornheart Coven Series (witch romance)
- Return Of The Fae Series (paranormal post-apocalyptic, completed series)
- Paranormal Criminal Investigations Series (urban fantasy mystery)
- MatchMater Paranormal Dating App

Series (paranormal romance, completed series)

- The Necromancer Council Trilogy (urban fantasy)
- Standalone Stories From the Paranormal Council Universe

Other Series

- The Apprentice Of Anubis (urban fantasy in an alternate world)
- Untold Tales Series (fantasy fairy tales, completed series)
- The Dragon Duels Trilogy (urban fantasy dystopia)
- ME Contemporary Standalones (contemporary romance)
- Standalones
- Seven Wardens, co-written with Skye MacKinnon (paranormal/fantasy romance, completed series)
- Tales Of Clan Robbins, co-written with L.A. Boruff (urban fantasy Western)
- The Firehouse Feline, co-written with Lacey Carter Andersen & L.A. Boruff (paranormal/urban fantasy romance)

- Kingdom Of Fairytales Snow White, co-written with J.A. Armitage (fantasy fairy tale)

Twin Souls Universe

- Twin Souls Trilogy, co-written with Arizona Tape (paranormal romance, completed series)
- Dragon Soul Series, co-written with Arizona Tape (paranormal romance, completed series)
- The Renegade Dragons Trilogy, co-written with Arizona Tape (paranormal romance, completed series)
- The Vampire Detective Trilogy, co-written with Arizona Tape (urban fantasy mystery, completed series)
- Amethyst's Wand Shop Mysteries Series, co-written with Arizona Tape (urban fantasy)

Mountain Shifters Universe

- Valentine Pride Trilogy, co-written with

L.A. Boruff (paranormal shifter romance, completed series)
- Magic and Metaphysics Academy Trilogy, co-written with L.A. Boruff (paranormal academy, completed series)
- Mountain Shifters Standalones, co-written with L.A. Boruff (paranormal romance)

Audiobooks: www.authorlauragreenwood.co.uk/p/audio.html

ABOUT THE AUTHOR

Laura is a USA Today Bestselling Author of paranormal and fantasy romance. When she's not writing, she can be found drinking ridiculous amounts of tea, trying to resist French Macaroons, and watching the Pitch Perfect trilogy for the hundredth time (at least!)

FOLLOW THE AUTHOR

- Website: www.authorlauragreenwood. co.uk
- Mailing List: www. authorlauragreenwood.co.uk/p/mailing-list-sign-up.html
- Facebook Group: http://facebook.com/ groups/theparanormalcouncil
- Facebook Page: http:// facebook.com/authorlauragreenwood

- Bookbub: www.bookbub.com/authors/laura-greenwood
- Instagram: www.instagram.com/authorlauragreenwood
- Twitter: www.twitter.com/lauramg_tdir